Enjoy!.
Chavis

D1396809

ADOPTING TIGER

by Chavis Fisher

Published by INdyPrint

11205 Lebanon Road, Suite 70
Mt. Juliet, TN 37122

Published by INdyPrint

INdyPrint books may be purchased for educational, business or sales promotional use. For information please write to: 11205 Lebanon Road, Suite 70, Mt. Juliet, TN 37122.

Cover Art by Jay Durrah
Library of Congress Cataloging-in-Publication Data application in progress.

ISBN 13: 978-0-9994560-0-2

First Edition

PRAISE FOR *ADOPTING TIGER*

Excellent story from start to finish! Chavis Fisher has brilliantly combined her professional prowess with her talent for storytelling. "Adopting Tiger" nails what I believe represents a true story of children who are circumvented by the family law system. This thrilling novel, which can be read in just one sitting, guides us through the twists and turns of an adoption battle for a very special child, Tiger. Chavis uniquely implements real-life human frailty. Will Tiger find the family he desires? The saga continues. A definite must read!

—Curt Randle El, Professional Athlete Wealth Advisor and Former Indiana University Football Player, Pittsburgh

Chavis Fisher hits on just about every aspect of the child welfare system in her book "Adopting Tiger," and I am amazed at how fluidly she does so. The story is not only interesting, but it is compelling. This book should be read by anyone who is touched by the life of a child and by any athlete who has been touched by an off-the-field issue.

—Gregg Ellis, Former University of Michigan Football Player and Child Advocates Chief Program Officer

The author takes a big swing and captures the struggle of two drastically different families - hitting a homerun in the process! This short and impactful novel will cause you to question yourself and struggle with what is best for Tiger. Chavis Fisher does a commendable job hanging Tiger's future in the balance. She keeps you at the edge of your seat - wanting to read more and more. Chavis strikes a chord with several issues all readers will relate to as she guides us through the highs and lows of family life. Job well done Chavis Fisher!

— Jermaine Ross, Former Purdue University Football Player and Retired NFL Player

Truly captivating! "Adopting Tiger" delivers a heartfelt, yet drama-filled storyline that will continue to linger with readers long after the final page. This narrative sheds light on the emotional roller coaster experienced by children in the foster care system - while simultaneously crafting dynamic characters and subplots which are highly relatable. Though Tiger appears to be the character that brings all of the others into focus, each individual has an interesting life or has unresolved past issues which make them equal contributors to the gripping plot. "Adopting Tiger" does a commendable job of exposing how un-confronted issues of one's past can manifest into instability within a family structure. Furthermore, the novel puts into perspective how well children are able to navigate these various terrains. This one is a must read for so many different reasons!
—Ebony T. Lee, PhD., Atlanta Educator

Chavis Fisher has penned a winding mystery novel; it's not about murder, espionage, or drug cartels. The drama deals with adoption. In this cleverly written work, readers get a low-level view of a rarely covered subject in our modern, high-speed lives—the tangled world of legal adoption and foster care complicated by family dysfunction. Enlightening readers with her vast experience as a family services attorney, the author weaves a masterful tale, casting her readers into the reality of legal wrangling between families, social welfare agencies and human propensity for pettiness which creates a ping pong ball existence for helpless children caught up in the labyrinth of court hearings, legal delays, and obfuscation. It is a world that leaves children dangling in the despair of uncertainty.
—Brian H. Settles, Adoptee, Author of *Smoke for Breakfast: A Vietnam Combat Pilot's Story* and *Shattered Dream*

Chavis Fisher brilliantly enlightens readers on the foster care adoption process in the creation of an amazingly entertaining story.
—Cynthia Newman, Author of *Raising Queens*

◆

To every child, young and old, who has been faced with, risen out of or is still maneuvering through life's pain and healing process.

FOREWORD

When Chavis Fisher asked me to write this forward, I was thrilled. I have known her both personally and professionally for over 30 years and I cannot imagine a better person to tackle this subject matter!

Adopting Tiger is a legal-thriller that will have you captivated from the beginning. Chavis Fisher, through the lives of a professional football player and a rising young football phenom; does a magnificent job highlighting the emotional ups and downs of family life. This book will provide readers with an in-depth exploration of the multi-faceted aspects of imperfect families. It unravels the internal and external pressures of the adoption process and of life in general.

From the first page, Chavis Fisher makes you feel an emotional connection with Tiger McKenney, the DCS system and families who care for children.

Adopting Tiger does a phenomenal job illustrating that athletes in professional sports are not immune to off-field issues and often have difficulty confronting obstacles in personal life, which ultimately threatens careers and inner tranquility.

This work is brief, complex, compelling and, most importantly, well-needed. I am looking forward to the next book in the series.

— Joyce Thompson-Mills,
NCAA Associate Director of Enforcement

PROLOGUE
Braxton, Virginia
February 2016

T iger hears voices, he thinks, one deep and barking and the other steady and somewhat soft.

Arising from his vertical sleeping position, he wipes caked gook from his barely opened eyes and stares at the blinking digital alarm clock. It's a blur. He flickers his eyes and gains focus, albeit dark focus. Tiger moves to the edge of his floor-rooted twin sized mattress and watches as "3:15 am" screams bright red from the clock. Tiger shakes his head quickly side-to-side, as if doing so will wake him from a dream or at least make the voices, the confusion, go away. His stomach rumbles with nerves.

Tiger's room is just about the size of a one car garage and is almost as cold. Pale on-again- off- again blue-green paint mostly covers the walls and ceiling. It's a wonder a twin mattress and dresser fit in such a small space, but they do. Tiny spider webs decorate all four carpeted corners and most of the ceiling. Mildew can be smelled through the multiple layers of stagnant Febreeze.

The female voice, now recognizable to Tiger, is that of Denise Hamner, Tiger's DCS, family case manager. *She must be in the kitchen.* Fortunately for Tiger, he's had the same Department of Child Services worker since he entered the Braxton Ward system, a feat to which not every child can brag.

She delicately calls his name. Tiger wants to answer, but is too scared; so he sits in silence, with his feet flat on the ground, his knees bent and his hands placed on the edge of the off-white mattress. One hand brushes across an old urine stain created by the foster child occupying the mattress before him. Curling himself as small as possible, he edges to the back corner of his bed. Cowering against the wall, Tiger pulls his threadbare top sheet over his head. A spider crawls across his arm; he doesn't dare swat it. If he can't see anything, then nothing can see him. He closes his eyes and hopes for the best.

Bits and pieces of conversations sneak under the door. "I didn't do it," exclaims a relatively high-pitched male before the clink of handcuffs. "Heeee's heeee's noooot here," slurs Tiger's foster mother, Maggie. A loud, dull thump momentarily quiets the four room house. *She must have fallen again.* He opens his eyes and peeks through the crack in his doorway in perfect view of the kitchen. At five foot two, weighing about one hundred and fifteen pounds, Maggie needs help getting back onto her kitchen barstool. Instead, police officers cuff her.

A bright white flashlight from outside forces its way through the delicate tan sheets draping Tiger's bedroom window and meets him directly in his eyes. He squints them open. "Got 'em," a male police officer shouts to another officer also scanning the outside of the house. Tiger closes his eyes again. If he can't see them, they can't see him. He tugs his sheet tightly overhead and sneaks a glance through a large hole. Three vehicles approach the driveway with flashing red and blue lights and running sirens. Two police cars, already parked, are silent.

With increasingly heightened nerves, Tiger pauses, voluntarily interrupting his pending upchuck. He hates throwing up. Control of his bladder is an opposing story. Tiger can't help but smell the urine now running down his barely caramel colored calf. Tiger, at twelve years old, has the athletic physique of an upper class high schooler; the academic mind of an A student; the emotional development of a traumatized eight-year-old and a love of football as strong as a human's need for oxygen. He feels the liquid warmth trickle down to his foot. Tiger loses control of his stomach. Vomit splatters everywhere.

Now, nearly drowned out by intermittent sirens and the elevated voices of blue uniformed men and women, Maggie's bumbled verbiage from the kitchen is slow, yet belligerent. A female officer, about six foot one and gentle, slowly opens Tiger's bedroom door and peeks her head inside. She gingerly walks forward - stumbling to gain footing, Tiger timidly staggers across the heavily spotted, short shaggy carpet in the direction of her welcoming arms. He almost nicks his eye on the police officer's gold star metal badge when she wraps her arms around him.

Tiger wishes he could feel at ease, feel safe. The problem is he doesn't really know what it means to be "at ease," at least not outside of Mama Paula's nurturing love. Mama Paula is Tiger's "in between" foster placement home. Tiger does, however, know this "it's time for a new place to live" drill more than he would like. Maggie is Tiger's third placement in the three short years he's been in the foster care system. Prior to Maggie, Tiger was placed with a pre-adoptive foster family who almost adopted him. The family filed documents with the court and even told Tiger about a final hearing date. But, everything stopped when his adoptive mother and father could not negotiate the DCS financial subsidy they needed to care for him. Tiger wasn't overly concerned. He then moved in with Mama Paula for a long stay which he loved. Mama Paula doesn't adopt children. She just provides love and care for everyone who comes into her home. *What's another place to stay? Maybe I'll get to go back to Mama Paula's. Maybe I won't.* Tiger's eyes well up with tears.

With one hand placed onto Tiger's shoulder, the police woman slowly escorts him into the kitchen. His heart races. Tiger runs into the wooden door frame and slightly bumps his head. He wonders if anyone can smell his urine or can notice the vomit on his red t-shirt.

Seated in one of the plastic chairs surrounding Maggie's small kitchen two-person table, is her boyfriend, sporting blood-shot eyes. His small dilated pupils blankly pierce forward. The boyfriend's skin is pale, yet flushed. Pink and red bumps complete his face.

In the middle of the table, Tiger notices white powder, a couple of razors, a needle and about three or four prescription bottles. Tiger must have slept through another party. At the edge of the table sits a smoky, oddly shaped glass tube. The familiar smell almost causes him to barf again.

Standing at five foot six even, and almost as wide, chocolate brown, Denise looks him in the eyes and says, "Hi, Tiger." She grabs a towel from the counter and hands it to him. Tiger wipes his mouth. The police woman removes her hand from Tiger's shoulder and Denise moves towards him. Tiger drops his chin while a few tears spiral down to the floor.

"He's been placed in three foster homes," Ms. Denise gently whispers to the officer. "He's probably triggering." Surprised someone has any idea how he feels, Tiger raises his head and lifts his hand to wipe more tears. Tiger doesn't quite know what "triggering" means, but he's pretty sure it describes him. *But why am I being removed again? Will I stay at the same school? Can I still play football?* His heart pounds so loudly, he wonders if anyone can hear it.

"It's not bad here," Tiger blurts out. Ms. Denise looks at him and smiles. She drops her chin and hugs him. The female officer tilts her head with understanding and grins.

"Did I do something wrong again?" Tiger asks Denise. *Or is it the dope I told my school counselor about when she asked why I smelled funny?* Denise doesn't answer.

Leaning into the female officer, Denise

whispers, "He always thinks it's his fault." She cups Tiger's ears, "His bio mom makes him feel that way." The officer raises her eyebrows. Denise pulls her navy purse strap onto her shoulder and leans in further. "What's her deal?" asks the officer. Denise shrugs her shoulders then responds. "You got me. She even blamed Tiger when she got caught leaving him and her baby nephew at home alone." The police officer takes a deep breath. "Yea," Denise continues, "The only way she got caught was because a neighbor lady found the eighteen-month-old walking down the street in only a diaper."

"Wow," says the police officer, grabbing the stick holstered on her waist, "I wish that was the first time I heard that story…" Denise shakes her chin up and down, tilts her head and rolls her eyes in agreement. The officer cups her mouth and whispers, "How long has he been in the system?"

Denise shifts, "About three years. He first came in when he was nine after his principal asked him about bruises on his back." Denise pauses, "He told the truth. DCS just did a safety plan though. He came right back home."

Denise goes on, "Tiger loves his mother, but is a little relieved the Judge stopped Breanna's visits a while back. She quit trying to maintain sobriety and ditched her outpatient treatment." The officer nods then looks outside. Two male cops motion for them to come. The sun is beginning to rise. Denise directs Tiger to step ahead of her. She continues to talk to the female officer, "When she would show up to visits, she was mostly under the influence." A bird chirps. Denise notices Tiger is listening. "It's just as well," she says, "he's tired of wondering which visits Breanna will actually show up to and which ones she won't." Tiger stares in space. He's shivering cold, but doesn't ask for his jacket. No one notices.

Ms. Denise reassures Tiger, "We're taking you to another home, but first, we're going somewhere special." She winks as she grabs the green heavy duty trash bag containing Tiger's things. His football falls out of the bag. Tiger rushes to pick it up. Looking at Ms. Denise, Tiger asks, "Am I still being adopted?" She opens the car door and motions for Tiger to get in the passenger's seat. "I hope so. You're a good kid ya know." Tiger likes hearing he's a good kid.

Thirty minutes later, Tiger recognizes the long gravel road Ms. Denise turns onto and he moves to the edge of his seat in anticipation; swelling at the thought of seeing his beloved emergency placement, Mama Paula.

Situated just inside the county line on the edge of miles of farm hills, Mama Paula's twenty-seven-hundred square foot two-level lays on three and a half acres of open land. Two rescue horses freely roam inside white wooden gates. Sensing Tiger's presence, and maybe even his heaviness, the horses swiftly approach the gate closest to Ms. Denise's parked car. Tiger waves in their direction, "Hey there, Dorothy-Ann. Hey there, Roscoe." He hears their feet pound the ground and watches both kick up dirt. Dorothy-Ann lifts her head and shows her teeth. The sun is rising.

Mama Paula is the closest thing Tiger ever had to a real mother, or at least to someone who loves him like a real mother. Even when

Tiger doesn't stay with her, Mama Paula finds a way to visit with him. No matter his home placement, she offers to take him to school and to his extracurricular activities. Because of Mama Paula, Tiger gets to go to the same school and keep the same friends and football coaches. Mama Paula enjoys being a constant in his life. Plus, it's her way of always being able to make sure Tiger is okay. Mama Paula opens the screen door with her famously warm smile, "Come on in, Boy," the sixty-seven-year-old dark chocolate woman with dark grey eyes motions. "Cat got your tongue?"

Mama Paula's salt and pepper hair lines her smooth skin. At first glance, one might not guess she's even over the age of fifty.

Mama Paula pats Tiger's forehead and pulls him into her oversized bosom for the best "grandma" hug he could get. Another boy comes down the stairs and gives Tiger a towel and the bag with all the temporary toiletries he'll need to shower. "Hurry up now," Mama Paula says, "We've gotta be at the church for my senior saints meeting in just a little while."

Tiger smiles.

"You still playin' the drums, right?" she asks. Tiger nods and runs up the stairs to shower and change.

Denise places her hand on the door knob, "I'll be back in a couple of days, Tiger," she yells up the stairs. She thanks Mama Paula and closes the door behind her.

While upstairs, Tiger vividly remembers the very first time he came to Mama Paula's. Only a day after he arrived, he overheard Ms. Denise tell Mama Paula, Tiger had to leave and go back to Breanna because of the safety plan. Little did Tiger or anyone else know at that time, Mama Paula's home and heart would be Tiger's safest place. After Tiger changes, they leave for church.

Mama Paula, Tiger and the boy enter the small, red and brown brick church building while the ten member men's choir is singing "….But I have found a Saaaaavior, and He's sweet I know." Tiger feels at home in church. He stares at the drum set and hopes he gets a chance to play. After the senior meeting, the choir director hands Tiger the drum sticks. Delighted, he plays for ten minutes straight and then they head home.

Early the next morning, Mama Paula calls for Tiger to come downstairs. His middle school football and former Pop Warner Coach is on the line. Tiger answers a few questions then hangs up the phone. Mama Paula is in the kitchen making breakfast. "Mama Paula," Tiger yells from the family room, "You know we're on Fall Break, but Coach asked me are you still gonna take me to winter football practice?" She yells for him to come into the kitchen. Tiger goes to the kitchen and repeats his question.

Mama Paula fixes her dark grey eyes into Tiger's hazel eyes, "Of course." Tiger asks Mama Paula if he can feed Roscoe and Dorothy-Ann. Mama Paula shakes her head. He runs outside. The horse caretaker gives Tiger a shovel first and points to the dung. Tiger throws his head back and smirks. He shovels for twenty minutes and then fills the horses' pails with hay and concentrates of oats, barley and corn. Tiger tosses in a few apricots for a treat. Dorothy-Ann seems to smile. About an hour later, the caretaker and Tiger mount up the horses and go for a ride.

Wind blows through Tiger's hat. The dirt is tight, but not too tight. The horses know the path, so they lead.

Later that night after football practice, Tiger, Mama Paula, and the boy play a game of Phase10. Tiger beats them both two out of three games. Later, he sits on the couch and watches Mama Paula rock back and forth in her chair as she knits clothes for foster babies who come into her home directly from the hospital.

Four days later, Ms. Denise knocks on Mama Paula's door. She chats a while then lets Tiger know it's time to leave.

Tiger grabs his trash bag of belongings, gives Mama Paula the biggest hug he can muster, and walks out the door. Realizing he forgot something important, Tiger drops his bag on the front porch. He runs back inside. "Almost forgot." He winks at Mama Paula and grabs his football.

Playing football is the one constant in Tiger's life. He hopes he never has to give it up. According to the Braxton Newspaper, he's pretty good at it, too.

On the way to only God knows where,

Tiger is silent. Ms. Denise looks at the football on the floor in front of Tiger's seat with a secret smile, and then asks, "What do you like about playing football, Tiger?"

Tiger pauses a moment and says, "I like to out-think the other guys. And I like being a quarterback."

Denise lays a high school football scouting magazine onto his lap and points to his name. "Braxton's Own Phenom: Meet 12-Year-Old Tiger" reads the caption above his picture. Tiger is the first middle school student to be recognized by the magazine. Denise has always known there is something extra special about Tiger; something about his ability to thrive in the best and worst of circumstances. *It's amazing he's been able to maintain any consistency despite all his disrupted homes.*

All the hoopla seems odd to Tiger. He just likes to play ball and he's done that since he started Pop Warner at six years old. Tiger would often hear people watching him say, "That kid is going somewhere." The magazine article quotes a Division I coach, "There's only a one and a billion chance this athletic genius won't make it to D-I."

Tiger doesn't know what "phenom" means and is afraid to ask. He does know he wants to make it to Division I and then to the Professional Football League. *That's my ticket outta here.* Once he makes it, Tiger wants to find his mother, get her off drugs, and buy her a house.

Denise and Tiger drive for another forty-five minutes, mostly in silence. Ms. Denise pulls up to a large black gate, whispers something to the guard and then punches some numbers into a square dial pad. Tiger perks up as they enter inside the gate. He's never seen a gate that moves on its own. *Is this a castle?* His eyes widen, scanning the perfectly manicured yard after yard. He looks out of the rear window and watches the gate close. *This feels like something on TV.*

Ms. Denise pulls into a long winding paved driveway. She softly honks a hello to a little girl shooting a basketball at the end of the driveway. The little girl waves and goes inside the mansion. Per Ms. Denise's instructions, Tiger gets out of the car and follows her up ten carefully red bricked winding steps outlining a waterfall. Denise rings the doorbell.

"Whaaaaaat...wait...whaaaat."

Tiger places his right hand over his mouth to keep from screaming. In partial disbelief, he looks up at the man answering the door and stares directly into the eyes of Braxton PFL legendary quarterback and home town star, Thomas Newman.

CHAPTER 1
Newman Estate
May 2016

"**D**o you want to adopt him?" asks six feet five, two hundred and thirty pound Thomas as he, Sonya and their two children sit on the taupe leather L-shaped sofa. It's Sunday morning at 11:00 am, so Tiger is at church with Mama Paula.

Sitting almost high and protruding through clear skies, the sun shines brightly into the family room. It exposes Thomas's olive skin. His sandy brown hair frames his rugged face and nose, just slightly crooked from being broken one too many times. Thomas is the premier Quarterback in the league. He's arguably the best-ever and, by just about everyone's account, has sealed a future spot in the Professional Football League Hall of Fame. Thomas eats and sleeps football, which has served him well. But, football doesn't fill all his voids. He needs something else, something with deeper meaning. He and Sonya both need something else. So, they decided to foster children. Thomas's father was a foster child and Sonya loves to care for those in need. As each year goes by in their marriage, Sonya and Thomas grow more and more apart. Sonya loves Thomas, but feels lonely when he's not around; which seems like most of the time. Thomas notices her distance. She's not as excited about games or box offices; and it seems like she's not as excited about him. *Maybe adopting Tiger will make them closer.* At five foot ten, Sonya is every man's trophy. Her naturally tan skin is to die for, and a lot of people actually do die from melanoma skin cancer trying to get what she has. Sonya's size DD breasts didn't come cheap, but well worth every penny Thomas spent as they salute him in perfect halt.

Sonya looks at their two children then at Thomas. All four smile and nod in agreement. "We're adopting," Sonya says.

Eight-year-old Dotty walks towards her

father and sits on his lap.

"Daddy, will you still love me?" she asks.

Thomas looks down as Dotty's rosy freckled cheeks and grins as he nods his head.

TJ - Thomas Jr., but no one ever calls him that - asks no questions. His twelve-year-old dark blue eyes, he gets from his mother, stare directly into his father's, "It's the right thing to do, dad."

Thomas is proud of his kids and their willingness to share their life with Tiger. Even though Thomas is the city's star quarterback and the family lives amongst the Braxton elite, Thomas has made extra effort to help the children understand the importance of giving back.

Several years back, when the town heard the Newmans were becoming foster parents, many wondered whether they had a "Moses" complex. They thought Thomas and Sonya wanted to rescue poor, broken children only to make themselves feel good. That doesn't matter to Thomas. Sonya, on the other hand, is a little more concerned with appearances, so she finds herself always explaining how she and Thomas are just "good people, doing the right thing."

Thomas has grown fond of Tiger and Tiger has grown fond of him. Tiger doesn't dislike Sonya and he loves his new brother and sister.

To Tiger, the Newman home almost feels like Mama Paula's. The longer he stays, the more he wonders will he *really* be adopted.

Just as the family finishes discussing the adoption, Tiger walks in with Mama Paula. "Hello, Mama Paula," says Dotty. Mama Paula flashes a grin. She stays and chats a few minutes then excuses herself to head home.

The rest of the afternoon is easy going. TJ opens a cherry wood chest and pulls out Monopoly and Dotty rolls her eyes as she pulls out a deck of Uno cards. "You got to pick last time," she whines as she looks at TJ."

"Tiger, we're going to play a game. You choose," says Sonya. Tiger picks Monopoly.

They set the board down onto the table with all its pieces. It's Sonya's turn to roll the dice. A call comes in to the cell phone sitting face-up at her side. She glances at the phone and taps ignore. Ten minutes later, the phone rings again. Sonya doesn't answer and turns

4

the volume to silent. She faces the screen to the floor. Thomas doesn't know whether he should be bothered. He marks it in the back of his head, but says nothing. The family plays Monopoly for the next three hours. At the end of the game, Thomas looks at Tiger and says, "We love having you here. And we've been talking. Is it ok if we adopt you?" The words ring music into Tiger's ears. Tiger stands up and wraps both arms around Thomas. For a brief second, he lays his head onto Thomas's shoulder. TJ joins the hug, then Dotty, then Sonya. They break apart and dish out high-fives. Tiger and TJ leave to play video games.

The next morning, Thomas calls Denise. "Hello," she answers. "Hello Denise, we've made our decision."

"O.k?" Denise says.

"We're going to adopt Tiger."

Denise affectionately gasps. She can tell from her monthly visits Tiger is flourishing in the Newman home. *Looks like he might finally get his forever family!*

"Great, Mr. Newman! Glad to hear it." Denise says.

"What do we do next?" asks Thomas.

"It's time for you to obtain an adoption attorney," she responds.

You'll want one who is familiar with the foster care system because these types of adoptions are a little different than private adoptions."

She provides him several referrals.

Later that evening after the kids fall asleep, Thomas and Sonya sit at opposite edges of their king sized bed. The windows above the bed board are slightly ajar and the wind strongly whistles through. Thoughts about Sonya's phone calls from yesterday whistle almost as loudly. "Babe, who was that who called you?" Thomas asks.

"Uuuum, when?" Sonya stutters as she looks away.

"You know, yesterday?" he says. She shifts her weight from left to right, "Oh that was my mom. She knew we were doing family time. I don't even know why she called." Thomas picks up the remote and turns on the television. *I'm probably over-reacting.*

* * *

The Lawyer
Later That Week

Thomas and Sonya pull into the parking
lot of the office of the adoption attorney they
selected, Sandy O'Day. They take the elevator
to the sixth floor. Sandy's office is small yet
productive. When they arrive, Sandy looks up
from contents of the manila legal sized folder
she's holding. She pushes her glasses to the
top of her nose and says, "Welcome."

They walk in.

"Coffee?" she asks.

She points to the pot to the left of the
doorway brewing fresh coffee in calming
rhythm. The fragrant vanilla bean scent
permeates the air. Sandy offers them a seat in
two chairs facing her desk. They oblige.

Thomas looks above Sandy's head and is
duly impressed with her mounted degrees: a
silver-framed Bachelor of Science in Business
degree from Purdue University, a gold-framed
MBA from Wharton and a double-sized Juris

Doctorate from the University of Braxton.

Sonya hands Sandy their completed intake packet.

As Sandy peruses through the documents in the packet, Thomas's eyes focus on a wall mounted framed picture collage of Sandy and all her adoptive families.

"What do you say, Thomas?" interrupts Sandy.

He startles, "About what?"

Sandy and Sonya giggle.

"About the name change. Do you want any parts of Tiger's name to change after the adoption?"

"Of course," says Thomas. "His last name to Newman."

Sandy makes a note and explains she will draft an adoption petition and collect their filing fees. She will then file the petition on behalf of the Newmans with the Braxton Probate Court.

"The Probate Court is different than the Braxton Juvenile Court, where all of Tiger's monthly neglect and abuse hearings are held," Sandy explains.

Sonya asks Sandy about Tiger's biological

parents and they play into the adoption.

"According to an earlier conversation I had with DCS, both their parental rights have already been terminated," Sandy responds. "So we should have no worries there."

Sandy sifts through her emails to double check. "It looks like Tiger's father is deceased and his mother's rights were involuntarily taken by court. I'll have to check to see whether the mother appealed her termination," Sandy explains.

"Sandy looks Thomas's direction and asks, "What about adoption subsidy?"

Thomas looks at Sonya then looks back at Sandy and asks, "What is that?"

"Subsidy is useful for most families," Sandra explains. "It's a federal government program which includes Medicaid, legal fees reimbursement and a post adoption monthly stipend."

Thomas wrinkles his forehead.

Sandy continues, "While every district uses its own process to administer the stipend, the Braxton DCS offers an opportunity to negotiate the amount based upon income and expenses."

"We're okay," says Thomas. Sonya chimes in, "We haven't taken money from the state to foster him, so we definitely won't take any to adopt him."

Sandy tilts her head, "I understand and it's totally up to you."

Sandy leans forward and continues, "Okay, so we should be able to proceed pretty quickly since the parental rights are terminated and we are not negotiating subsidy. We just need to file your adoption petition and ask DCS to file its adoption summary and agency consent. We can then obtain a final hearing date and believe it or not, the Probate Judge will make a ruling right then and there. As long as there are no snafus, you and Sonya will walk out of court as legal mom and dad."

Both Thomas and Sonya's eyes widen in excitement. Thomas places his hand on Sonya's knee, "This is real, now."

Sonya's phone vibrates in her purse. She reaches down inside and hits ignore.

CHAPTER 2
Clarissa Moore
May 2016

Clarissa, Breanna Moore's estranged half-sister, and by some accounts, self-appointed family matriarch, opens the wooden doors to the 3,000 square foot domicile she won in her divorce settlement. She plops her 5'3" frame down on the egg shell white cushioned sofa.

Flipping through the pages of her 2016 financial plan, provided as a one-time complimentary service by her company's employee outreach department, Clarissa notes she is ahead of her income forecast. Clarissa has worked for the same company for fifteen years and has proudly reached her goal of a $72,000 annual salary. Her multi-level marketing company adds another $3,000, and the year is not even half over. Spousal maintenance, which unfortunately ends in

December, and child support should round her to about $100,000. Clarissa glistens in satisfaction.

Clarissa's appearance is unassuming, yet consistent. She doesn't believe in fussing much over what to wear or what others think. Some might call her plain; Clarissa calls herself practical. To look at Clarissa, one would know she is mixed, or at least suspect. Clarissa relates most to the black side of her family, although she gets along with the white side just fine.

Clarissa opens a box of chocolate chip cookies her diet forbids and turns on the tube. She laughs at the "You're So Lazy and Mean" episode of her favorite teletherapist show. She can relate to the guests who "work from home," yet double as helicopter moms. Clarissa dismisses the popular psychologist's theory of enmeshment and self affirms she's doing just fine "not having a life for herself outside of her children." *And no, I don't alienate my children from their father.* After the show, she changes the channel to a reality station. Clarissa is thankful she's worked for the same company the majority of her adult life, a company which seems diametrically opposed to firing people for lack of productivity. As long as she logs into her computer before 9:00 a.m.; logs out after 5:00 p.m. and does a little work in between, the higher ups don't bother her much.

She continues to look through her financial plan and stumbles across a smaller folder. She opens it and notices a copy of the petition she filed to adopt her nephew, Tiger McKenney. Attached to it is a copy of the interview sheet she completed for an attorney she didn't hire several months earlier. No, she's never met Tiger, but what difference does it make, he's her blood. Clarissa's "no good" sister, Breanna, breeds children like a jack rabbit in uninterrupted heat. She's not "no good" because she's an elite breeder and at thirty has birthed more children than a person can count on one hand, but because she's a heroin whore who continues to bring drama into their already drama-filled family: strange men, stolen property and yes, the Department of Child Services.

The first time Breanna got involved with the Department, she was fifteen and an emergency room doctor discovered several deep skull fractures in her then, six month old child's head, while treating the baby's nonstop seizures. Breanna, of course, denied knowing anything about it and was ordered by the Court to undergo drug and alcohol treatment and to take anger management classes. She did neither. The baby girl was adopted by someone the family barely knew. No one has seen or heard from the adoptive parents. The last thing Clarissa heard is they may be in Ohio with her niece. Then, there are the twins, both born with heroin in their system. It highly upsets Clarissa no family members have seen them since they left the hospital with a DCS social worker. It also upsets Clarissa no one else in her family has ever stepped up to adopt or care for any of Breanna's kids. Breanna is not her favorite person, and Clarissa has two boys of her own to raise, but, Clarissa believes she has to step up and try to adopt Tiger.

Clarissa remembers the day she heard, through the family grapevine, DCS took Tiger – and the day she learned he was an exceptional football player. The story goes that a teacher noticed a three-inch bruise on his back, knee, or something and that Tiger claimed he got it from falling down the stairs. *Breanna has no stairs.*

Another one of Breanna's children, the one Tiger seems to be closest with, was recently removed from her when the four-year-old boy told the day care provider one of Breanna's "friends" touched him in bad places. Clarissa and Breanna's sister, Jeanean, told Clarissa, Breanna didn't believe the child until she found the "friend" mounted on top of a neighbor girl's six-year-old body with his pants down and a gun to her head, beckoning her to stay still until he climaxed. There was already semen on the floor.

Clarissa is not necessarily interested in cleaning up Breanna's messes and never really considered adopting any of her other children. Clarissa has to admit she is a little intrigued with the football attention Tiger receives around Braxton, and she figures Tiger needs to be with his biological family anyway. Clarissa knows her siblings will think she's a hero for saving him from the system.

Clarissa grabs the cell out of her purse and calls a number she was given by Jeanean. It's the telephone number for Denise Hamner.

Denise answers, "Hello."

"What do I need to do to go forward with this adoption for Tiger McKenney?" Clarissa asks.

"Excuse me, who is this?" Denise responds.

"This is Clarissa Moore, Tiger's aunt...and I have already filed my petition to adopt Tiger. I just want to know when it'll be final."

The phone goes as quiet as Sunday service in the Methodist church. *Shit*

Denise regains composure, "And your lawyer?"

"Still looking for one, I filed the adoption petition on my own," responds Clarissa.

"Ma'am, I need to call you back, what's a good number?" Denise asks.

Clarissa provides her cell number, and they end the conversation.

Denise calls the Adoption Court and sure enough an adoption petition has been filed by Clarissa to adopt Tiger. She asks the Court Clerk to forward a copy.

Denise takes a look at the petition, and

sees it is signed by Clarissa and not signed by any attorney – Clarissa filed *pro se*.

Maybe that's why I never knew about her.

Denise calls her DCS legal department. The attorney assigned to the case confirms he, too, knows nothing about Clarissa. He lets her know the adoption is now considered CONTESTED.

The Newmans and Clarissa have to fight it out in court, and the Judge will decide what's in Tiger's best interest.

Before Denise gets the chance to return Clarissa's call, Clarissa calls again.

"It's me, Tiger's Aunt," she says.

"Hello, Ms. Moore."

"Aren't you Tiger's caseworker?" Clarissa asks.

Denise does not immediately respond.

"What do I do next?" she demands.

"Well yes, Ms. Moore, yes I am and it's not quite as simple as it may look."

Clarissa sighs aloud, "Well, make it that simple."

"Pardon?" Denise responds.

She continues, "Ms. Moore, you need to hire an attorney, and he or she should be able

17

to answer your questions. From our standpoint, DCS doesn't even know who you are or whether you have a criminal history. We have to consent to your adoption, but we had no idea you filed an adoption petition until now..."

Clarissa rolls her eyes. "I'm Tiger's Aunt...his mother's sister. And that's about what you need to know."

"Ms. Moore, I have to tell you we're currently supporting another family in Tiger's adoption. He's bonded well, which has been hard for him to do. He's very happy where he is. Does that mean anything to you?"

Clarissa takes a sip of soda, "Uuum, I'm family. Does that mean anything to you?"

"Yes, and you've never met him or stepped up to adopt him or any of your sister's other children..."

"What difference does it make? I'm stepping up now. What do I need to do next?"

"You need to talk to your attorney; that's what you need to do." Denise hangs up the phone.

Clarissa calls back. "I think we got

disconnected."

"How may I help you?" says Denise.

"I need to know what all I need to do," blurts Clarissa.

"You have to be evaluated. After that, we'll make a formal recommendation. The Court takes it from there."

"Thank you," Clarissa hangs up.

Clarissa chuckles and turns down the television volume. She calls her younger sister, Jeanean, at work.

"Hello," answers Jeanean on the third ring in her uniquely raspy voice.

Laughing, Clarissa blurts, "They think I don't know who the 'other family' is. Shit, the whole town knows." Jeanean laughs.

Clarissa walks into her kitchen and opens the refrigerator. She makes a sandwich. "You know I beat them to the punch and filed first," she tells Jeanean.

Clarissa and Jeanean crack up and then catch up on the latest family gossip. Clarissa's face turns red with amusement when Jeanean mentions, "Mom just kicked Veronica out again." Veronica is the middle sister. *Always family drama.* Clarissa shakes her head.

Jeanean's dad keeps trying to call her, but there's no way in hell she will answer. Jeanean's memories of his emotional abuse are just not cute. She mourned the loss of a connection with him a long time ago.

Clarissa walks outside and crosses her yard. It's slightly raining and hazy clouds cover the sky. She opens her red and black brick-enclosed custom mailbox while Jeanean continues to chatter.

"Ohhhh lord, a letter from an attorney!" Clarissa interrupts.

Clarissa hurriedly opens the manila envelope decorated with fancy letterhead. Jeanean starts in on how Breanna is no good and doesn't deserve any of her children.

Just as Jeanean is spilling more beans about Breanna's life, Clarissa's pulls out the first page of a three page document from the envelope. She reads, typed on white paper with black ink, "Petition for Custody."

Clarissa's mouth drops open, and her head becomes lighter than skim milk. She races back across the yard, nearly dropping her phone, and punches through the door. Jeanean is still gabbing. Clarissa enters the front room and reaches for one of the love seat arms to steady her. She stumbles. Sweat drips down her forehead and accumulates at a sprinter's pace to her cheeks. Her face is flushed.

What the what?

Interrupting Jeanean, Clarissa stutters, "I-I-I just don't believe it."

Jeanean stops ranting. "Believe what?" she asks.

Clarissa blurts, "My ex-friggin husband just filed for custody of my boys. That idiot!"

"Wow," exclaims Jeanean, "he'll never get them, Clara," she encourages.

"I'm f–floored...I...I gotta go..." Clarissa's face is as red as an animal that has just bled out.

She ends the call before Jeanean can respond and bends her torso over her knees. She clinches her fists and screams.

* * *

About thirty minutes later, the school bus drops ten-year-old Jeremy off at the end of Clarissa's winding driveway. He throws his

21

school bag down on the multi-colored tile entrance floor and looks down to see his mom sitting on the ground with her back against the wall. She's staring into space. "What's wrong?" he asks.

"Your dad's an asshole," Clarissa snares.

"Mom, don't start that shit," spits Joseph, the eldest of the two as he enters the house. He's far less sympathetic to his mother than is his younger brother.

"Joey, I'm getting tired of you cursing at me," she yells.

He rolls his eyes and leaves. *Serves you right.*

A couple of minutes later, Clarissa walks down the stairs and enters her almost-finished basement. She gets on the treadmill and fires up a joint. The boys know to leave her alone.

CHAPTER 3
Thomas and Sonya Newman
May 2016

The next day, on the way home from Dotty's drama camp play, Thomas receives a call from Denise. Sonya encourages him to pull over the pearl black Land Rover to answer. Dotty sits in the back passenger seat with pink *Beats by Dre* headphones hovering over her small ears. Tiger and TJ skipped the play to go over a friend's house. The family dog, Chloe, however wouldn't have missed it for the world. She barks as the SUV stops.

"You're kidding me," Thomas mutters. He listens to Denise another ten minutes and hangs up.

Sensing Denise must not have given good news, Sonya questions him. Her white linen capris covering her sculpted calves shift as she crosses her right leg over her left.

23

Thomas explains about Clarissa and her attempt to adopt Tiger. His words are broken and weak.

Sonya's not ever seen her husband so bewildered and for a brief moment becomes a little jealous of Tiger.

Sonya calculates and places her hand on Thomas's shoulder. "The adoption is important, Thomas, but so are other things."

She unbuckles her seat belt and faces him directly.

Sonya wants to be the person at the center of Thomas's world and over the past few months, it looks like Tiger has filled the vacant space. He seems to be more bonded with Tiger than he is with his own children. Sometimes Sonya wonders what her life would be like had she never gotten married, had she never trapped Thomas with a pregnancy.

With watering eyes, Thomas shifts his head and looks into hers. "We have to tell him, Sonya. We have to figure it all out. We just have to tell him." Sonya fastens her seat belt.

Thomas takes the SUV out of park and

returns to the paved road.

Thomas has never backed down from a challenge and he doesn't intend to now. He changes his focus. "How's your mom, Sonya."

Sonya is thrown off guard. "She's great. The doctor says she's got a little vertigo, but on the whole she's good."

Thomas watches Sonya move like a gazelle as she explains. He's amazed at how she still turns him on.

Dotty leans her head on the window and falls asleep as Chloe lies in her lap.

Thomas is worried about the adoption, but he tries not to show it.

He loves Tiger like his own blood. In addition, his competitive juices have kicked in. Thomas hasn't lost too many times in his life. *What if we lose and don't get to adopt Tiger? What will happen to Tiger with an aunt he barely knows?*

Thomas pushes the thoughts out of his head. He hasn't lost too many times in his life, a ball game maybe but on the whole, the stars in his universe are always in perfect alignment. This is a time they need to line up again.

Over the next thirty minutes, the car is quiet. Thomas reflects on his historical dominance, his sheer ability to rise above anything which has ever come his way.

He thinks about his college career. Though few believed he could, Thomas mixed his natural athleticism with a lot of head strength, sweat and tears to capture the starting Varsity Quarterback position as a true freshman. Thomas went on to break more conference and national records than any other player in the university's history. His drive, work ethic, cerebral prowess and confidence make him the best at everything he does.

He further contemplates the day when his father left his mother, him, and his siblings. Thomas was just fourteen; yet he stepped up and became the man of the house. He's had zero regrets.

What if this time the universe doesn't line up?

He needs a distraction. He finds one - the sweet smell of Sonya's perfume.

Thomas turns to Sonya, "What's Clarissa's angle?" Sonya's shoulder length brown-blonde hair shifts as she shrugs her shoulders.

"There's no doubt we've got more love for Tiger than she does. He doesn't even know who she is...I I...I know he's only been with us for a short...but, he's a perfect fit. And he's doing so well with us."

Sonya is hurting too, well sort of. She enjoys Tiger, yet wonders how he feels about her. She decides a show of empathy is needed.

"I know Tommy. We've read everything we can, and we have the top adoption attorney in the State. We're going to be fine," she assures.

Thomas makes a right into the neighbor's driveway to pick the boys up. Tiger and TJ run out of the house. Chuckling, they jump into the two seats next to a now awakened Dotty. Chloe jumps onto Tiger's lap. He pulls out his phone and shows TJ a Snapchat video of a school girl he likes. They chuckle more. The image disappears. Dotty takes off her head phones and shakes her head.

Sonya is right, the adoption is important, but so are other things, like Thomas's upcoming contract negotiations. He's three years into a four-year deal with the Bears. Thomas is approaching his biggest incentive clause yet. If he sets the all-time passing record within the first four games, he'll be paid an unprecedented $30 mil - making him the first quarterback in the PFL to do so in such a short period of time. Based upon his stellar career performance and the lump sum the Bears could be out of, Thomas and his agent, Dopp, know this is a good time to renegotiate. Sonya wishes he was so strategic about his marriage.

Sonya's phone rings. She thought she had it on silent. Her eyes dart quickly in Thomas's direction. He's chatting with TJ about what girl he likes. "Hey there, Mom. I have to call you back later. We just picked up the boys," she explains to the caller.

CHAPTER 4
Braxton Department of Child Services
May 2016

At the DCS main office, Denise stares towards the white baseboards. She can't stand to hear the whiny nasal monotone sound coming from her Division Manager, Rob. It's as if he's a chronically sick piece of chalk.

Stale coffee brews in the back corner of the dry conference room. Denise, Rob and Denise's supervisor, Sheila, are the only people seated around the large table. Denise is ready to empty herself right out of the chair. Sitting for the last two and a half hours, she's been forced to give a summary of each of the forty-three cases in her load.

Denise has more cases than any other social worker in the county and wonders if it's her punishment for blowing the whistle a year ago on Sheila. Sheila had approved the return of a baby in DCS's care to his biological mother without thoroughly checking his file. The biological mother previously admitted she hears voices and one such voice told her to drown her baby. She never received psychological treatment. The young child lived only seventy-two hours after he entered his mother's care. Officers found him alone in a car at the bottom of a man-made lake. Why Sheila was not fired is an anomaly.

Denise grabs the pen from behind her ear and accidentally touches the life size American flag behind her. She wishes for her own freedom right about now. The flag slightly obscures the framed portrait of President Barack Obama. Directly below is the unobstructed picture of DCS Executive Director, Randy Governs—*typical DCS*.

Denise sips her coffee. The bitter taste assaults her taste buds. She secretly dribbles it back into her red and white DCS "Children First" mug.

After discussing a few quick admin cases, Sheila pulls out an unusually thick file.

"How about the Tiger McKenney case?" she asks Denise.

Denise squeezes her blue foam rubber stress ball. Tiger's doing exceptionally well in the Newman home, so she has no worries there. The only thing that concerns her is the part of the file she lost containing medical records and background checks. She's done everything she can to duplicate, but knows there are gaping holes.

Denise was once a top-tier family case manager on the fast track within the agency. Somewhere along the way she lost her zeal, not all, but some. Years of stress, politics, lack of appreciation and general bull has gotten the best of her. And she's not the only one. DCS case manager turnover is at an all-time high. Half of Denise's current cases have already passed through the hands of at least two, sometimes three other social workers. Some of her files are complete with progress reports, court orders, and evaluations and some of her files are embarrassingly dry and empty.

And people wonder why things slip through the crack,

Denise searches the bottom of her stack of papers.

"What have you found out about Clarissa Moore?" Rob asks. Denise proceeds to sort through her notes, which are unfortunately a bit sketchy. She's got most of it in her head though. Sheila seems to notice and writes something down on her pad of paper.

"Well," Denise says, "I'm still gathering information, but from what I can tell Clarissa is the sister of Tiger's mother and has two children of her own, both boys. Workforce development shows she's employed at a large cable company. Further investigation shows she works from home."

"We need to do a staffing," says Sheila. Denise doesn't know what a staffing is, but is afraid to let Sheila and Rob know. She squeezes the stress ball now positioned on her lap beneath the table.

Denise figures by the look on Sheila's face, she knows Denise doesn't know what a freaking staffing is. Prior to now, Denise has had less adoption cases than she can count on two hands, and none were contested. The majority of her cases have been emergency removals and high intensity placements. It seems as if every time Denise gets the opportunity to experience the lighter side of social work, Sheila snatches the case and hands it off to a less seasoned worker. Denise is muddling her way through Tiger's adoption contest. Actually, she and Sheila both are muddling their way through as Sheila has never had a contested one either. They go over her remaining files and then break for the day.

Denise knows she must get on top of her game. She plops down in her medium cushioned cubicle chair. "This is the first time I've had two families attempting to adopt the same child since I've been here," Denise tells her new cubby mate, Roxanne. "What's a staffing, and how do we do it?" she whispers.

Her blank look says it all. Roxanne has the same clue Denise has—none. Denise misses Jody, her old cubby mate; Jody always knew this kind of stuff. *Why did Jody have to go and have a baby?*

Denise searches the DCS internal portal for the word "staffing" and finds:

> DCS "Forever Family Staffing"
> is a process used, in contested

adoption situations, to determine to whom the DCS agency will give consent. Both families are thoroughly evaluated through an in-office interview or a "staffing." During the process each party is questioned about their adoption motivation, personal background, strengths and weaknesses, future planning, and parenting style.

Denise sifts through the more than forty pages of DCS adoption policy and calls Thomas to schedule a home visit as soon as possible. She prints off the finger print forms Thomas and Sonya need to sign ASAP.

CHAPTER 5
The Staffing
One Week later

Denise pulls into the Newman driveway. It's a bright hopeful seventy-five degree day with only a few clouds in the sky. She turns off the tunes from the local smooth jazz station and gets out of her baby blue Ford Fiesta. Birds chirp rhythmically in the background only to be interrupted by the on-again-off-again sprays of water from the various sprinkler systems. A neighbor waves as he passes by in a decked out golf cart with his wife. His teenage son follows driving a separate cart.

Unlike many of her other cases, Denise looks forward to her visits at the Newman's home, not just because of their upper-class lifestyle and all their material trappings; but mainly because Tiger now is doing the best she's seen him do over an extended period of time. No outbursts have been reported. His nightmares have ceased, and he smiles more, a lot more. Tiger is working well with personal tutors and gets to experience more than either he or she could dream. Tiger is set to go with TJ to a weeklong robotics camp at Vanderbilt later in the summer. After that, they will attend a behavioral economics camp for a week at Stanford.

Denise rings the door bell and is greeted by Dotty's bright smile. "Deniiiise," she screams before jumping into her arms. Dotty wraps her arms around Denise's waist. Denise grins and half-carries-half-drags Dotty across the foyer into the family room where everyone else is waiting, lounging on the floor. Tiger sees Denise and laughs; but won't open his mouth. His face turns dark red.

Denise sets her purse down, "What'd I miss?" she asks.

Dotty points to Tiger and then runs over to him and tries to tickle him. He rolls on the floor, but doesn't give-in.

Chloe passes loud gas and Thomas and the kids burst into laughter. Sonya is at her mother's house and should arrive any moment.

Thomas tries to trick Tiger by talking about a girl he knows Tiger likes. Tiger still doesn't open his mouth. Denise looks at Tiger, "Cat got your tongue?"

"Show her," TJ encourages.

Tiger slowly allows his lips to purse open broadening his smile and displaying one metal brace after another, top to bottom.

Denise is thankful Tiger is able to get braces. It's yet one more benefit he receives by living with the Newman's as Medicaid, the only state issued health insurance for foster children, doesn't cover braces.

After Denise plays one round of Uno with Dotty, Thomas, TJ and Tiger, Sonya enters the house. She hangs her keys on a wooden wall rack. Denise asks Thomas and Sonya if they can speak in private.

"Upstairs kiddos," Sonya motions for them to get up. Tiger calls dibs on the family gaming system. All three race up the stairs.

Denise moves to a kitchen bar stool beside Thomas and Sonya. "You know I found out more information about the aunt that's contesting your adoption." Denise looks away, "I'm not supposed to be saying anything, but I so believe in you, I'm willing to take just a little risk." She looks Thomas's direction. "You haven't heard anything from me, right?"

Thomas and Sonya both nod "yes."

"Do tell," says Sonya.

Denise uncrosses her legs. "Well, from what I can see, it looks like Clarissa is a divorced single mother." She sets her purse on top of the blue and green granite island. "She's Breanna's oldest sister, but it doesn't seem like they have the greatest relationship."

Sonya exits the bar stool and offers Denise a cup of orange juice. She accepts and continues, "There are other siblings, most of which have been in the DCS or criminal system for one reason or another. None have stepped up to care for any of Breanna's children. This is the first time Clarissa has shown any interest in Tiger. He's been in the system for three years and she never even asked to visit him. Interesting thing is..."

Sonya taps Denise's arm and interrupts, "I have a friend who works for the Braxton Superior Courts. She pulled Clarissa up in their system. It looks like her ex-husband just filed custody papers for their sons."

Thomas narrows his eyes. Unsure why Sonya hasn't mentioned this to him, he chimes in, "I wonder what that's about?"

Denise shrugs her shoulders "She's a single mother who might lose her own kids. I'm no lawyer, but that's not a good look."

"Will that help our case?" Thomas asks.

Denise takes a sip of juice and clears her throat. "I'm thinking so," she responds. "The Court will look favorably on the family that gets our DCS nod of approval."

Relieved, Thomas asks, "What's our next step?"

"To show up to the 'Forever Family Staffing' next week, with bells and whistles," responds Denise.

* * *

The next week Thomas and Sonya show up to the staffing at the Braxton DCS office seemingly calm and ready. They take the offered seats in the small conference room and answer a myriad of questions from Sheila about their respective childhoods. Thomas skips over the fact he was molested by an uncle when he was ten; a memory he's successfully pushed to the back of his mind. He does admit, though, his father left the family when he was a boy.

Sonya briefly zones out and fights off thoughts of the many men who failed to commit to her, including her own father. He couldn't remain loyal to her as a dad or to her mother as a mate. Sometimes he was present, but even when he was, he wasn't.

"And what do you do for discipline?" Rob chimes in.

"Redirect, we redirect," Thomas answers.

"What do you do for fun with Tiger?" asks Sheila.

"We try to have a family game night each week and really just hang out," Thomas asserts. "Tiger and I toss around footballs, baseballs, basketballs…you name it."

"Why do the two of you want to adopt?" asks Sheila.

Thomas looks at Sonya, and Sonya looks at Thomas. Thomas proceeds, "We feel we can help heal his wounds. Sonya and I have been together a while and have nothing but love and stability to give."

The interview lasts over an hour and ends with Rob telling Thomas and Sonya DCS will meet with the other adoption candidate and get back to them with its decision.

An hour later, Clarissa arrives. She accepts the coffee offered to her by Sheila and takes her seat. "Can you tell us about yourself, Ms. Moore?"

"Yes," she quickly responds. "My name is Clarissa Moore; I have two boys and a stable home…" For twenty minutes she explains why she should be chosen to receive DCS's consent. She mentions nothing about her custody battle.

Rob looks up from his notepad, "Why do you want to adopt Tiger?"

Clarissa sits on the edge of her chair and demands, "Tiger should be with his family."

"Is there anything you want to know about your nephew?" Sheila questions.

"No," Clarissa responds. "I just think once he gets to know me, he'll be just fine." She's satisfied with her answer.

Sheila asks again, "Are you sure there's

nothing you want to ask?"

Clarissa can't think of anything, so she smiles and again says, "No."

Rob goes on to explain the staffing process and ends the interview just short of an hour.

"Thank you, Ms. Moore," he says.

"Is that all?" Clarissa asks?

Sheila responds, "We've already met with the other family. We will get back in touch with you as soon as we have made a decision."

Clarissa stands up and exits the room.

* * *

Thomas and Sonya head home anxious and confused, yet hopeful. They stop for a bite to eat on the way.

Soon after Thomas pulls into the garage and closes the door, Denise calls them with the news. Their family has been chosen by DCS to adopt Tiger. The committee believes Tiger has bonded well with the Newman's and to remove him now would be way too traumatic. Furthermore, the committee feels the

Newman's, unlike Clarissa, put Tiger's needs ahead of their own. DCS will draft its agency consent and file with Court right away.

Thomas buries his face between his two hands gripping the steering wheel. He tries not to let Sonya knows he's crying. She acts like she can't tell, but she knows. Thomas gathers himself, leans towards Sonya in the passenger seat and kisses her on the cheek.

Thomas and Sonya burst through the garage door leading to the house. Tiger and TJ hear the commotion and run down the steps. Thomas grabs Tiger and picks him up with the biggest bear hug he can muster, "You're going to be ours, son."

"Thomas…" interrupts Sonya, "It's not done yet. We still have to go to court."

Thomas ignores her.

Tiger doesn't hear Sonya. All he hears is Thomas's voice calling him "son."

Tiger sleeps all the way through the night for the first time he can remember. *I'm going to be adopted!*

CHAPTER 6
Newman Estate
June 2016

Early in the afternoon, Thomas grabs his Nike gym bag from the couch and throws his Samsung cell phone inside. He goes upstairs and changes into his Braxton Bears gray and blue cotton practice shirt and dark blue performance shorts to get ready for 1:00 p.m. strength and conditioning at the Bears' complex.

While in the master bedroom upstairs, Thomas hears a faint vibration. He checks his shorts pocket for his cell phone. *It's downstairs.* He hears the vibration again. Thomas runs downstairs and sifts through his bag for his phone. No calls have come through. He runs back up the stairs and stands in the middle of the walk-in closet. He hears the vibration again and again. It stops. It starts. He traces the sound to a dresser drawer, Sonya's dresser drawer. Thomas opens the drawer and discovers a brand new iPhone delicately placed inside a winter sock. The phone is locked. He can't look at the call list. Thomas is running late. He yells for Sonya. She doesn't answer. He places the phone back inside the drawer.

Speeding out of the driveway, Thomas almost hits a neighbor's golf cart. He calls Sonya. She doesn't answer.

After strength and conditioning, Thomas receives a call from his agent.

"Tommy boy," says Dopp.

Preoccupied, Thomas answers, "Hey."

"How's Tiger?" Dopp asks.

"He's well."

"Listen, I'm not going to keep you. Our negotiation is looking good. We should be able to finalize something in July before summer camp," says Dopp.

A contract is the last thing on my mind.

Dopp is one of the top three agents in the PFL. He's known to negotiate top dollar contracts latent with strong, carefully calculated performance incentives. He's never let Thomas down, and he trusts Dopp with all his business affairs. He's shrewd, yet ethical. Without Dopp, Thomas would not have built his endorsement dynasty or executive produced any of his television shows.

Today just isn't a business day.

CHAPTER 7

Preliminary Adoption Hearing
Braxton Superior Court, Probate Division
One Week Later

C larissa has only been inside a court
room a few times in her life. She's not
looking forward to it.

The court halls are as stale as three-week
old bread and the stench far worse. She can't
find the Probate Court.

Clarissa gets on a west wing elevator. It
goes down to the basement. Seemingly faint at
first, a urine aroma intensifies as Clarissa
walks in the direction of the, now open, steel
door entrance to the County lock-up holding
cells. Clarissa looks ahead and sees five
African American men in orange jump suits,
chained together by their ankles, all fighting to
walk in unison. What seems like a "chain
gang" to Clarissa is being escorted by two
fully suited guards, one on both ends. For a

brief moment, Clarissa feels the prisoners' despair, an unfortunate familiar emotion from her past.

"Ma'am, may I help you?" the first security guard asks Clarissa.

"Yes, I-I-I'm looking for the Adoption Probate Court," she says.

"You're heading the wrong direction." He points her to the main entrance of the court enclave as the chain gang passes. The stench is deafening, and Clarissa nearly barfs.

Five minutes late, Clarissa opens the door to the court office and checks in. She's escorted by a brown uniformed bailiff to the seat next to her newly hired attorney.

Inside the courtroom, a floor to ceiling red, white and blue American flag hangs to the right of the Judge's mahogany, freshly polished bench and stands at a fluid halt.

"All rise," says the bailiff, as Judge Estolia enters and takes his seat.

Judge Estolia sits in a magnificently over-sized black chair camouflaging his black robe. At about three hundred and fifty pounds, he is a larger man than most, which explains the extra-large chair. Below him the court reporter sits poised to record. The bailiff takes her seat to the left.

Clarissa and her attorney sit at a small table facing the Judge. Thomas, Sonya and their attorney sit at the table facing the judge to the right. Clarissa's allergies have been acting up lately. They seem to get worse when she's nervous. She sneezes. The fresh lemon furniture polish still wet on the wood in front of her doesn't help. She sneezes again.

"Bless you," the Court reporter says. Clarissa smiles a "thank you."

Court doesn't seem to have officially started as the Judge, the bailiff, and the reporter all stare at their computer screens.

The clock on the wall directly above the Judge Estolia's bench ticks loudly and as slowly as a fruit fly in a glass of apple cider vinegar.

The Judge finally raises his gavel, clears his throat and says, "Court is now in session in the matter of 47-D09-1406-05658, In re: the adoption of Tiger McKenney."

Clarissa's palms sweat as she places them laced on top of her lap. Her white shirt is creased. Her dark navy paints, however, are wrinkled and as out of place as she feels. She focuses straight ahead. Even though she feels justified in what she is doing, Clarissa briefly wonders whether she will really win the adoption, especially after DCS informed her she was not chosen for its consent.

Thomas glances toward Clarissa. Their eyes meet; they both blink then look away.

Thomas is accustomed to not showing nervous energy; he's had to master that skill his entire football life. Thomas's dark blue custom tailored Armani suit fits his tall physique to a tee. His white shirt and blue silk tie accompany nicely. Thomas runs his extra-large fingers across his freshly straight razor-shaved face and whispers to Sonya who's decked out in a coordinating suit.

Judge Estolia motions to both attorneys and asks if any settlement agreements have been reached. Clarissa looks away sternly. She has no intention of settling for anything, other than full parentage of Tiger.

Thomas doesn't flinch. He and Sonya have no idea who Clarissa is or whether she's loony. They certainly take issue with the fact Clarissa's husband has filed for custody of their boys, which men rarely do. Sandra believes that's a point in the Newmans' favor. Thomas has no intension to settle.

Sandra clears her throat and responds, "No, your honor."

The Judge squints as he turns to Clarissa's counsel, "You're really going to make me have to decide this? This boy has been through enough, and you guys just can't figure it out."

The room is silent.

Judge Estolia peruses the electronic court file for what seems like an eternity.

"I'm ordering mediation to be completed within the next thirty days. A Pre-Trial hearing will be re-set then."

Judge Estolia slams his gavel on the desk, stands and marches out the courtroom.

"All rise," follows his bailiff.

* * *

Clarissa
Later that day

When Clarissa returns home from Court,

she calls her favorite uncle, Charlie. He always seems to know just what to say. Uncle Charlie is on the black side of Clarissa family and is her estranged father's brother. Uncle Charlie is the oldest of five siblings and is the closest thing Clarissa has ever had to a real dad. He is the only one she knows in her family who has stayed married; forty years and counting.

"It'll be ok, Clara," Uncle Charlie says from the other side of the phone. "Mediation can't be all that bad."

"I know," Clarissa says, "I just don't know who that Thomas Newman thinks he is...trying to disrupt our family." Clarissa plops on the bed.

The boys are gone with their father and his new wife for their midweek visit; and even though Clarissa fought it tooth and nail inside, she agreed in order to look good in custody court. She's actually kind of glad they're not there to bug her. *Besides, Matthew needs to get a taste of what he's asking for.*

"Well, Clara honey, a lot of this is Breanna's fault," says Uncle Charlie. Clarissa rolls her eyes. She knows he's telling the truth, but it just feels better to blame Thomas

Newman.

Clarissa, affiliating more with her black genes, doesn't believe in white families raising black children. She always felt her Caucasian mother didn't quite know what to do with her as a child, and sometimes wonders if because she is darker than her siblings, her mother values her less. Even though Tiger is "light bright," he's still mixed, which classifies him as black. Clarissa wonders if Thomas and Sonya even have the ability to teach Tiger what to do when he walks onto an elevator and white women clutch their purses.

"They have his hair so wild, Unc. I saw a picture...He looks like a little black-white boy."

"Clara?" says Uncle Charlie.

Clarissa receives a call from Matthew. She hits Ignore. Clarissa knows it's about time for the boys to return and Matthew is calling to see if she is home and quite frankly, she doesn't give a damn.

He wanted them, so he gets to keep them until I'm good and ready.

Uncle Charlie changes the subject, "What's going on with the custody stuff,

Clara?"

Clarissa explains she's got to go through some Domestic Relations Counseling Bureau, evaluation.

"What's that?" he asks.

"My lawyer, the same one for the adoption, says the DRCB is an agency appointed by the Braxton Superior Court to assist the Court with custody battles like ours."

"Oh," he responds.

She continues, "I guess they evaluate both me and Mathew and write a recommendation on who should get custody of the boys. *It seems like the DCS staffing all over again.*

Clarissa has gone through one of interviews and let the evaluator know Matthew is a piece of shit who only wants the boys because he just got married.

CHAPTER 8
Braxton, Matthew Moore
July 2016

"I Wonder if she's done her eval," Matthew says to his new wife Holly. He sits up in their King sized bed, "You know I didn't want to do this?"

Holly sits up and places her arm around his shoulder. She motions for him to rest his head on hers. "I know, Honey, but you had no choice."

Matthew is just now bouncing back financially from his divorce from Clarissa. By no stretch of the imagination, though, does he mind the marital maintenance or child support he has to pay. He'd rather take a hit to his pocket than the continued hit to his person he experienced over and over while married to Clarissa. Clarissa is not a bad person; she is just so darn volatile and unpredictable. There seems to always be a demon she chases. It's just hard to keep up with which one.

Early in their marriage, Matthew noticed the coldness with which she treated some of her family, but he never thought the maltreatment would boomerang back to him. Towards the end of the marriage, he often had to remind himself of something his mother always told him before her death: "Son, no one can outrun their character. It just can't be done."

With the storm window above their bed ajar, the sound of the whispering wind and the smell of the drizzling rain merge in unison. Matthew rubs his forehead. "I'm tired of only seeing the boys when Clarissa gets a wild hair up her behind and allows me to....and this is when they need me the most."

"You don't have to explain it to me," says Holly, "I live it every day,"

Matthew raises his head. A few tears trickle down his face. Holly catches one and wipes it away. She holds him again gently, yet tightly.

For some reason, Matthew never felt this comfortable with Clarissa. He never sensed he could cry or be truly vulnerable. Most times, his tenderness was met with Clarissa's detachment sprinkled with her sometimes-biting sarcasm. "You're a little soft," she would say. "What man cries?" she would taunt.

All Matthew ever wanted to do in their marriage was make Clarissa happy. *If I just say yes to what she wants, she will be happy.* It took him a long time to realize how truly wrong he was. During the marriage, he often retracted into a shell and his softness with Clarissa was short lived.

Not surprisingly, Clarissa has nothing positive to say about Holly. What she says most is that she doesn't want Holly anywhere near her children. Matthew is convinced Clarissa is threatened because the boys both slipped and called Holly "mom" in front of Clarissa a while back. Other than that, there really is no reason.

When Holly first came into Matthew's life, she reached out to Clarissa so that Clarissa could meet the person who was around her children. Clarissa played nice at first. They even exchanged numbers. After about three months, Clarissa started sending Holly unsolicited paragraph long text messages about what gifts she can and cannot give the boys and what activities she could and could not attend. Because Holly refused Clarissa's adult parenting, Clarissa no longer speaks.

Matthew finally returns the boys home. He's excited he has another visit coming up with the boys this weekend and he's surprised Clarissa agreed again. Maybe, it has something to do with the custody battle.

* * *

That Saturday, Matthew turns his car engine off and waits for the boys in Clarissa's driveway, his old driveway; the same driveway he used to teach each of his boys to skate board, to ride bikes. Matthew shuts off his walk down memory lane before it goes too far; before he gets lost. He calls them twice, but receives no answer. It's a little unusual, so he wonders, but not too much. He can't let his imagination get the best of him. Matthew turns the air conditioner to high and waits and waits. He decides to go to the front door and ring the bell. Matthew opens his car door and steps onto the pavement. Sweat runs down the back of his blue shirt. Eighty-three degree heat illuminates from the overhead sun piercing through a cloudless sky. Matthew hopes this visitation pick-up will be uneventful, but he doubts it will be. He rings the doorbell.

Matt knows Clarissa's got to be pissed as hell, not because she doesn't want the boys to see him; he believes she does. But because she wants his visits to happen on her terms and her terms only. That's mostly at her house or when she can come along. Clarissa seems to really enjoy when the four of them are together, which makes Matthew wonder why she filed for divorce. True they were separated, but they were still working on their relationship, and still screwing from time to time. Matthew was willing to go to counseling. She told him to go to hell.

There was once a day, even after the divorce, Matthew believed including Clarissa in his visits was the only way he could see his boys. So he, now regrettably, obliged. These days, however, Matthew's gained an ever hardening back bone and is progressively growing a pair of steel balls. His requests now are for time alone with the boys.

As Matthew's balls have grown, so has Clarissa's denial of his requests, at least before he filed for custody. She would often claim the boys have school projects, extracurricular activities and mandatory activities with her family. Ever since Clarissa was served with papers, she has granted all visitation requests.

Jeremy answers the door. Clarissa is right behind him in her bath robe. She rolls her eyes at Matthew, kisses both boys, and then slams the door.

They drive silently to the baseball game.

The closer they get to the stadium, the more the boys begin to talk. Excited to see the Braxton A's minor league team play in the new downtown stadium, they roll down their windows and stick their heads out. They go through security and look for their seats. After they find them, they gladly plant on the hard, silver metal benches; Matthew and the boys grab hot dogs and cotton candy. Fresh popcorn permeates the air. On the announcer's cue, the three sway in unison and sing, "Take me out to the ball game..."

"She's so into this adoption, she doesn't even think about us," Joey blurts out of nowhere.

Jeremy motions for him to shut-up.

"We haven't even met this kid, Tiger," Joey continues.

"Neither has she," adds Jeremy. I-I mean mom is great. I just wonder."

Matthew doesn't let on that he's just as perplexed.

Clarissa has always tried to outshine her sisters as if she was the one that has it all together, and he wonders if this is her motivation. Or, maybe she just truly wants to love this kid. He doesn't want to spend too much time trying to figure it out. He learned a long time ago Clarissa is complex, not all bad and not all good, just complex.

"Plus she's always gotta control everything," says Jeremy.

"What do you mean?" asks Matthew.

Joey sighs, "Dad, you know."

For some reason, Matthew begins to feel sorry for Clarissa. *What a miserable life. You must be miserable to act the way she does.*

61

The game is over and Matthew takes his sons to grab a quick bowl of pasta before he takes them home. Sensing Jeremy and Joey do not want the time to end; he makes a stop at the twenty-four hour arcade near their home. He calls Clarissa to let her know, but she does not answer. He leaves a message. At about 11:00 p.m., Matthew pulls into Clarissa's driveway. He feels tension from the boys, no maybe nervousness. Matthew can't quite put his finger on it. Jeremy holds in a whimper.

Matthew keeps the car running and opens the doors for the Joseph and Jeremy. He walks with them to the front porch.

"Dad, do we have to stay here?" Joey whispers.

"She's got this new boyfriend," Jeremy adds. "His name is Dagger, and he doesn't like us at all." Matthew's eyes widen.

"And she's always yelling," says Jeremy.

"Boys, I'm working on it. Just give me some time."

Clarissa swings open the front door. Matthew is sure neighbors on both sides can hear it as it slams against the brick wall. He instinctively checks to see if it is off its hinges.

Clarissa pushes Matthew in his chest. Jeremy grabs Clarissa, "Moooom, stop."

"Who do you think you are bringing them in so late?" she barks.

"I called, Clarissa, and you didn't answer," Matthew replies.

After a five minute tirade, Clarissa says, "And where were you last night? Once again the boys didn't see you at their game. Her face is now red. "I'm surprised you didn't show up. There shouldn't be anything more important than *your* boys."

Matt lowers his head and places his hands on both sides of his temples.

"You didn't tell me they had a game, Clarissa. I just found out tonight. How am I supposed to know if you don't tell me? I don't even know what summer leagues they're in. And you make sure they don't tell me, telling them not to talk about what's going on inside the home." He turns to the boys. "Please go inside."

Matthew lowers his voice to an almost whisper and leans in, "You have them scared to death."

"I still can't believe you didn't show up,"

Clarissa screams.

It takes everything Matthew has inside of him not to call the mother of his children a "Crazy Bitch."

He clinches the fists at his sides, "I'm getting tired of it, Clarissa."

"Tired? You're not too tired to get a new wife and some big house on a hill."

"Whatever," says Matthew.

"Whatever. From now on you'll find out about the kid's activities from them."

"Clarissa, they are ten and twelve years old... whatever," he says.

"Whatever, whatever," says Clarissa as she pushes Matthew again and slams the door behind her."

"Deadbeat!" she yells through the door.

"Cuckoo!" he responds. Matthew leaves and calls the boys on the way home to make sure they are okay.

CHAPTER 9
Clarissa Moore
The next weekend

Clarissa is dressed in a grey sweater and traditional cut Levis. She gets cold easily. She pulls her Toyota Camry out of the two car garage, opens the door and yells for the boys and Dagger, her new boyfriend. Joey and Jeremy come out in their red and blue practice shorts and matching Nike back packs containing their basketballs and tennis shoes. Dagger is cool as a cucumber with a black and white heavy metal tee and slim fitted jeans. His brunette wavy hair just hits his shoulders.

Clarissa slams the car door shut. "Boys, I'm going to ask you one more time, you don't want to live with your father, do you?" The boys are on their way to summer basketball practice for one of the three teams of which they are apart, the only one their dad knows about.

"Clara, you keep asking the same question," Dagger points out. Clarissa met Dagger during her not-quite-divorced period. He wasn't so divorced either. Besides that, they seemed to be a good fit.

"Who asked you?" Clarissa glares at Dagger before turning to Jeremy. "You are not to talk to your dad about anything that goes on in this house. Do you hear me!" She tells the boys that when their dad picks them up from practice, they are to tell him that they enjoy their school friends and that they don't want to live with him. At the end of the thirty-two minute lecture, she lets them out of the car. Through pursed lips, the boys mumble something Clarissa is sure had better not be profanity.

Still in the parking lot, Clarissa begins a ten-minute unilateral discussion with Dagger. "You're not their father," she says. "So you need to keep your mouth shut."

Just as Clarissa begins to pull out of the gym parking lot, she spots Matthew's car. Clarissa circles back around to her original parking space and jerks her car into park.

Dagger's head bobbles. Removing the key from the ignition, Clarissa tells Dagger to come with her inside the gym.

Clarissa suspects, actually knows, Matthew sees her and Dagger so she positions herself in the bleachers directly across the gym, facing Matthew. Dagger sits six inches away. And just in case Clarissa is wrong and Matthew doesn't notice, she screams a deafening "That-a-boy Joey," as he shoots an uncontested lay-up.

Clarissa catches Matthew looking her way and hopes he's jealous. She screams again. Dagger drops his head into his lap.

A half an hour later, Clarissa moves to Matthew's side of the gym, about three bleachers behind him. After setting her purse on the bleacher in front, Clarissa walks down to the coach's bench and pulls out the box with shirt orders and passes them to the parents in the stands. She's pretty sure all eyes are on her. The coach's wife gives her the side eye. She doesn't care.

Clarissa continues to pass out t-shirts. She turns to her left and spots Holly in the distance at the gym entrance. Holly sits down next to Matthew and Clarissa begins a not so quiet conversation with two of the single fathers. She hopes Holly and Matthew are listening and checks through the corner of her eyes. She doesn't care so much about whether Dagger is aware. Clarissa makes her way to the row directly behind them, leans forward and taps Holly's shoulder. "You shouldn't be here," Clarissa says.

Holly gently touches the spot Clarissa grabbed, looks ahead, and says nothing. The parents surrounding the drama smirk and pretend to concentrate on the scrimmage. The mother of the star Center giggles aloud. Matthew's face reddens with embarrassment. Holly places her hand on his knee in reassurance. Clarissa notices, "Good steal, Jeremy," she yells as the second string shooting forward blocks Jeremy's lay-up.

After the scrimmage, Clarissa motions for Joey and Jeremy. They drop their practice bags and meet her in the corner of the gymnasium. Joey and Holly high-five a couple of the boys' teammates and hug a few of the parents. Just as Matthew walks over to the Coach, Clarissa abruptly ends her conversation with the boys and waltzes over. The boys walk away from the drama towards Holly.

"Wow, you're giving him a game schedule," Clarissa exclaims to the head coach. Matthew just takes the schedule and leaves.

On Clarissa's drive home, she places her index finger on her temple and says to Dagger, "Oh, I forgot to do something." She calls AT&T and blocks Holly from Joey and Jeremy's cell phones.

* * *

Later, Clarissa and Dagger lounge on the soft carpet of Clarissa's family room floor, with a glass of Moscato. Dim lights set the mood. Extra-large couch pillows support them as they sit only inches apart. Clarissa enjoys having Dagger around. He's a little rough around the edges, and that excites her; reminds her of how she envisions her dad would be, had he been around. Matthew was boring and predictable and pretty much a pushover, at least until lately. Clarissa is sure his wife has something to do with that. While her sisters seem to care, Clarissa is not bothered that Dagger once had a criminal record, or still has a record, however that goes. It was a long time ago anyway. *A couple of minor marijuana possession charges at nineteen does not a bad person make.* He got off on some drug diversion program anyway and never even served probation. Dagger is passionate and a beast in bed.

Dagger leans in for a kiss. Clarissa moves toward him. Her phone rings. She looks down and sees it's Denise. Clarissa taps the green "answer" button and grabs a pen. "The mediation will take place at the Braxton Child Advocacy Center in uptown Braxton in a couple of days," Denise says.

Not the Braxton Child Advocacy Center. A flood of memories race through Clarissa's mind just like the roaches raced across the floor in her childhood home. Clarissa recalls her youth counseling sessions at the center. She especially remembers the times her mother showed up drunk and loud and the time her mother had to be escorted out by a police officer after she punched a social worker.

With tears in her eyes and while fighting off an anxiety attack, Clarissa looks over at Dagger, who is now sitting on the couch half asleep. *Thank God for Uncle Charlie.* Tears roll down her face. *Without him, only God knows where I would be.*

CHAPTER 10
Braxton Child Advocacy Center
Adoption Mediation
The Next Week

ive minutes before 1:00 p.m., Clarissa
parks in front of the red brick three
story Braxton Child Advocacy Center.
The smell of barbeque from a nearby rib joint
catches her attention. A stray pit bull going
through rubbish barks. The silver metal railing
running along the six outside concrete stairs is
wet from the sideways rain.

After getting off the elevator on the third
floor, Clarissa checks in with the mediation
receptionist and is buzzed into Room A.
Clarissa enters a small conference room with
eight seats placed around a long wood-like
table. The mediator, Karen, asks Clarissa to be
seated in the chair bearing her name tag.
Clarissa's attorney, Kent Kennard, is already
seated. He smiles and passes her the joint

confidentiality agreement for her review and signature.

Thomas and Sandy are seated directly across the rectangular table. Clarissa looks for Sonya, but doesn't see her. Clarissa's chair squeaks as she sits down. She views Thomas a little closer than she did in court and must admit he's one of the most handsome men she has seen. Denise and the Court Appointed Special Advocate sit in the chairs directly next to Clarissa's left. Karen stands to her right at the head of the table closest to the door. The DCS attorney sits, typing on his laptop, at the head of the table against the back wall.

"Where's Tiger?" Clarissa whispers to her attorney.

"He's not a part of the mediation," her attorney responds.

Clarissa thought for sure she would finally get the chance to meet Tiger and must admit she's disappointed when she doesn't.

"The juvenile court still hasn't granted your visitation, Clarissa. They haven't fully vetted Dagger's criminal history and until they do, we just have to wait," her attorney whispers directly in her ear.

"Let's get started," says Karen. Still standing, she turns toward Sandy, "Is Mrs. Newman joining us?"

"No," utters Sandy, "her mother is sick," she continues.

Karen begins with her introductory, canned statements about the process. "Mediation is a tool used by many courts around the country for the purpose of making good faith attempts to reach agreements between opposing parties. Adoption courts often order mediation before setting final hearings in the case of contested adoptions. The hope is that the parties desiring to adopt the same child will somehow agree that it is in the best interest of child that one party adopts and that the other party receives the right to some sort of post adoption contact. We must all make a good faith effort, and I will notify the Court only whether or not an agreement was reached and not about any details or any discussion which occurs in this room."

Clarissa shifts in her seat.

Thomas shifts as well.

Karen sits down, "Let's go around the

table and introduce ourselves." She motions to the opposite head of the table.

The DCS attorney looks up, "I'm Dan Snow, the DCS attorney assigned to the case." Karen motions to the next person. "I'm Denise Hamner, DCS family case manager." Karen grabs a white Styrofoam cup and takes a sip of water.

An office phone rings in the background.

"LaTasha Wise, CASA volunteer."

Karen gestures toward Clarissa, "Clarissa Moore, Tiger's Auntie."

Her attorney tightens his tie and scoots to the front of his seat, "Kent Kennard, adoption attorney for Clarissa Moore."

Sandra clears her throat. "Sandra O'Day, adoption attorney for the Newman family."

The clock steadily ticks. Thomas feels steady, Clarissa surprisingly does, too.

Karen looks Thomas's direction, "Mr. Newman what would you like to see happen today?" Everyone stares in his direction. Thomas pauses and takes a semi-deep breathe. "At the end of the day, we want what's best for Tiger. We would love to adopt him and if we could work out some sort of contact with Tiger and Clarissa after an adoption, we would be more than happy to have that." Clarissa gently rolls her eyes.

"Ms. Moore, if the Newmans were to adopt, what type of visitation might you agree to?" asks LaTasha.

"Full," says Clarissa.

"No, Ms. Moore, I mean how many times a year are you proposing you visit Tiger," she says.

"I intend to have Tiger full time," Clarissa responds.

Thomas maintains a game face.

"Clarissa," Denise says, "the Adoption Court will likely take issue that you have never met Tiger."

"Well then, I need to meet him," Clarissa responds, "When will that happen?" Clarissa's attorney taps her leg in a silent request for Clarissa to shut up.

"These aren't the people you want to piss off," he whispers in Clarissa's ear. "They have a lot of power."

"That's a no deal for me," Clarissa corrects. I want to adopt Tiger, and it's best he stays with his family."

For only the second time during mediation, Dan looks up from his laptop. "Thomas, how is Tiger doing in your home?"

Thomas unfolds his hands. "Awesome. Tiger and TJ dress alike most days and tell everyone they are real brothers. Dotty tags along and annoys like most little sisters do."

Everyone in the room chuckles. Even Clarissa cracks a smile.

"Clarissa," says Dan, "is there anything you want to ask Thomas about Tiger." Clarissa looks at her lawyer and responds, "I can't think of anything."

"Can you tell us about Dagger and what role he would play in the adoption?" questions Denise.

"He won't," Clarissa asserts. "He's just my boyfriend, not my husband."

After an hour and a half of back and forth, no agreement is reached.

Karen concludes, "I will make a report to the adoption court we could not reach a settlement and the court will then set a trial date. Unless an agreement outside of mediation is reached prior to trial, the Judge will determine which adoption is in the best interest of Tiger."

CHAPTER 11
Braxton Bears Training Camp
July 2016

Thomas wipes the dripping sweat from his brow, and cleans his hands on the white towel hanging from the back of his navy blue practice shorts. It's a beautiful eighty degree day. Well, not beautiful for Thomas and the rest of the Braxton Bears doing OTAs. It's hot as hell, birds chirping or not. Hard sweat permeates the air. Popcorn, too, as today is "Family and Media Day" at the Bears training camp.

OTAs, where players "volunteer" to attend non-mandatory practices, are thankfully coming to an end for Thomas. Previously, he thought about opting out, maybe to push himself past his "play by the rules-unwritten rules or otherwise" type of personality, but then thought against it. This just wasn't the year, not with his contract situation unsettled. *Or maybe it was.*

Thomas hopes to finalize a new contract before mandatory camp in a couple of weeks.

Thomas has to admit to himself, he's been so preoccupied with Tiger's adoption; he's pushed the contract negotiations to the back of his head. Dopp's on top of it, though.

The final whistle blows. Tiger and TJ lean over the metal practice field fence and wave at Thomas with excitement. Dotty, standing next to Tiger, wraps one arm around his waist the other around her mom's leg and shines a big smile in her dad's direction. The children have been looking forward to family media day for a while. They love seeing the other Bears' families and running around with the other kids to get their favorite autographs.

Sonya walks over to Thomas, who is now signing autographs inside the practice fence near the 50 yard line. Thomas gets a whiff of her Bottega Veneta perfume, his favorite. He bought it for her last Christmas. Sonya kisses him on his cheek and quickly shimmies the double DD silicones, filling her low cut, fitted light blue Bears football t-shirt. She turns and walks away.

A reporter from a prime time sports station rams a black mesh microphone tip into Thomas's face, "How about that record?" Thomas flashes the patent pearly whites and gives some expected answer about it all being a team effort.

Reporters, careful not to trip over the kids, young and old, running around collecting autographs, pour in from every major, and minor, TV network, blog, magazine and newspaper.

Most ask Thomas about his contract negotiations and pending All-time passing record. Under the old or new contract, Thomas's performance this year can translate to big dollars. But, the interviews revolve solely around the quarterback controversy.

In last year's draft, the Bears picked up a young quarterback in the first round. Thomas is only slightly bothered. He infectiously smiles at every insinuation.

In the sea of white media vans, bearing bright red, yellow, and blue colored call letters and large satellite gadgets, Thomas recognizes one of his least favorite reporters approaching and walks the other direction. The smell of the freshly cut grass tickles Thomas's nose. He rubs it. "How about that adoption, Thomas?" shouts the reporter. "I hear Clarissa Moore is giving you a run for your money."

Thomas ignores him. He heads to the locker room to shower and to get ready for the Bears family barbecue. Tiger runs up to him and cuts off his path. "Hey Dad," Tiger exclaims in excitement. Tiger offers a high-five. Thomas gives him one with each hand.

Thomas's heart melts followed by anxiety, but he doesn't want to show it. Will he ever really become Tiger's dad?

Tiger, wearing his white Newman replica jersey with big, bold letters, hands Thomas a football to sign for the foster kids at the advocacy center. Thomas pulls out his sharpie and Tiger puts the ball in the green netted sack with the others.

Tiger's white jersey highlights his sun-kissed, now, slightly more caramel summer complexion. Even though Tiger is biracial, he's milky light in the winter, and most people confuse him all year round for Caucasian or Other, but certainly not black. Tiger used to make it a point to let everyone know he is African American. It made him feel closer to his biological family that way. Now, he doesn't care.

"Where's your mom?" Thomas asks Tiger.

Tiger shrugs his shoulder and looks away.

Thomas calls Sonya a couple of times and leaves messages. *Maybe her phone is dead.* They head to the grill. Dotty eats her last hot dog and Thomas gathers TJ and Tiger from their flag football game, and they all head to the car.

Clouds begin to permeate the sky. Thomas turns on the kids' favorite pop radio station and zones out.

Thomas and the kids pull into the garage and the seat belt clicks as Dotty unbuckles hers first. Sonya meets them at the door wearing her favorite Braxton Bears apron and offers Thomas one of her piping hot homemade rolls. She smears her famous peach preserve onto Tiger's and it melts in his mouth.

Thomas smells a roast cooking.

"Dinner's almost ready, Honey." It's 8:30 p.m.

"We just ate," Thomas reminds Sonya.

"Oh, I know," she says, "I just wanted this for later. She unfastens her apron and tosses it on the bar stool. Sonya touches Thomas's shoulder, "Mom called me, Honey, and I had to run her to the doctor. I-I-I didn't have time to let you know. I'm sorry," she says

Sonya cleans a few dishes, "Game night," she yells to the children.

"I need to talk to you," says Thomas as he cuts his eyes.

"Daddy!" Dotty yells as she comes down the stairs, "come play a video game with us."

Thomas becomes paranoid. He wonders, then dismisses, and then wonders.

I wonder if the kids know anything. I wonder if I know anything.

Thomas's head aches.

Thomas wonders if the kids sense what he senses. *They can't. Not the kids.*

CHAPTER 12
Bank of Braxton
The next Monday

On the way to meet his Quarterback coach to look at practice film, Thomas pulls his jet black two door Porsche into the parking lot of the corporate branch of the Bank of Braxton. He parks just to the left of the silver and maroon "Reserved for Bank President" sign sitting above the space housing a sweet vintage baby blue drop top Cadillac Series 75. Thomas almost swipes the Cadillac door as he gets out. Off balance, he stumbles and almost sprains his ankle.

The architecture of the bank is unassuming, yet quaint. It's the oldest building in Braxton and still maintains its original 1868 English architecture. As he walks in to the entrance, Thomas smells the fresh grilled burgers and brats the nice lady in an apron has on a black barrel grill in front of the bank to commemorate customer appreciation day. Thomas grabs a burger. The blackened Cajun seasonings slide down his mouth. He holds the door for an elderly lady leaving the bank and accidentally bumps into the bank president, Harold Stone.

"Nice ride, Thomas," says Harold, Braxton Bank President, as he exits the building flashing his charming, yet somewhat insincere, smile.

Thomas goes directly to the office of the branch manager. While there, Thomas explains a discrepancy he's noticed in his account.

"Which account, Mr. Newman?" says the branch manager.

With his right eyebrow drawn high and his chin quickly tilted toward the floor, Thomas says, "Pardon?"

The manager pauses and punches a few buttons onto her keyboard. She points her index finger at the screen and calls her assistant manager into the office for verification.

With a frown, the manager says, "Mr. Newman, my mistake, it looks your wife's account somehow got linked to yours.

Thomas's complete body involuntarily reddens.

He feels a hit in his stomach worse than a Mack truck smacking an old lady. *Sonya has never had her own account. It's got to be a mistake.* Well, he hopes. Seemingly calm, Thomas looks outside the manager's glass window and sees two tellers pointing at him. They look away. More blood rushes to his head followed by nausea. His palms sweat and his bowels loosen. "Thank you," says Thomas as he rushes to the men's room. He momentarily gathers himself and exits the bank to his vehicle.

With both hands on the steering wheel, he Bluetooth voice directs his cellular phone to call Sonya. She doesn't answer her phone. *Bullshit. This is some bullshit.* He hangs up.

Strongly tempted to skip his meeting, Thomas heads over to the complex. He pulls into the parking lot and exits the car. He relieves himself in the men's room again. Film is the last thing on his mind.

Two hours later, Thomas leaves the complex - a little more calm, yet still somewhat on edge. During the drive, he calculates his next move. Thomas is kind of like that 500 Rummy card player who likes to wait until he has full spreads in his hand before he lays out – and when he lays out, he lays all the way out. *But this one is tough. It just doesn't add up.*

"Did you get my call?" he demands of Sonya as he enters the house. She shakes her head "no." He's sweating, but doesn't want to show her, at least not yet. She grabs her phone and shows him, "No missed calls."

Increasingly nervous, Sonya asks, "How was your day?" Thomas looks at her, but doesn't answer.

Sonya suspects something is up, but can't say for certain. "Dotty drew this beautiful picture of the family." Sonya hands Thomas a detailed 12x12 pencil sketch of Dotty, Tiger, T.J. Sonya and Thomas holding hands side-by-side.

"Nice," Thomas responds. Thomas walks to the kitchen island. Sonya follows. "I went to the bank," he says.

Now, Sonya's heart sinks. She composes herself, "Good, is Molly, the teller, still there?"

Thomas doesn't answer.

Sonya thinks quickly on her feet. *Guilt trip time.* "I've been meaning to talk to you Thomas. I don't know that I can take all the time you spend away from me and the kids much longer. I feel like I'm raising ours and another child all on my own." Thomas wrinkles his forward in confusion. *He fell for it. At least I think.*

Usually, when Sonya goes down this road Thomas recounts all the times he's at home and if it weren't for his job, which keeps him away at times, she wouldn't have nice things and the children wouldn't be in private school... But he refrains, "O.K."

Sonya really knows something is up.

She tries a different approach and screams, "You've never been good to me! You've always been married to football."

In shock, Thomas flashes back to the first time he met Sonya. She was a waitress at the Humidor cigar bar. He was "married" to football then and Sonya didn't complain. She didn't complain when he moved her out of her mom's trailer park or when he put a ring on it after she became pregnant. He stares at her with no expression.

Funny thing is, even though Thomas married Sonya because of the pregnancy, he has truly grown to love her.

"I see all the women who wait for you after the games." Sonya continues. She takes a breath, "You NEVER have time for me or the kids. You're the WORST husband a woman could have. ALL the other wives spend time with their husbands...but YOU...you're always at work...even when you don't have to be. I hate football and I hate you!"

Is this some reverse psychology bull? Is this woman really trying to make me think something is wrong with me?

Like a true legend quarterback, Thomas remains outwardly calm. Inside, he's ready to explode. He holds it in.

Tiger walks into the room, "Mom, Dad, my birth mom just instant messaged me."

CHAPTER 13
Clarissa and Matthew, Custody
July 2016

The adoption isn't the only thing on Clarissa's mind either. She sits in her attorney's suburban office. It's noon and the custody hearing is in a couple of hours. To make matters worse, Attorney Kennard just told her the Family Domestic Review Report recommends Matthew for primary physical custody and not her. She reads through the report and takes special note of a highlighted statement.

> Ms. Moore currently has primary physical custody of the couple's minor children. Mr. and Mrs. Moore share joint legal custody which requires them to make joint decisions regarding health, safety, education, religion and all

other major and minor facets of the children's lives. Ms. Moore consistently makes solo choices regarding the minor children and has gone over and beyond to alienate them from their father. Ms. Moore's distasteful parental alienation of Mr. Moore from his children's lives is unconscionable and is far from being in their best interest.

This Reviewer respectfully and strongly recommends the couple's minor children be immediately placed with their father and that he be granted sole physical and legal custody.

Clarissa throws the report down on her attorney's desk.

She tries to hold in the gas that's been attempting to pass from her uneasy stomach. She looks at her attorney now sitting on the other side of her desk directly next to her and she asks, "What does this mean?"

Her attorney looks directly in her eyes, "Well, it's only a recommendation, a strong one the Court will take into account, but a recommendation nevertheless. So we have to decide whether we want to fight it or whether we want to attempt to negotiate a settlement."

Clarissa pauses briefly, "Let's fight."

* * *

Matthew feels somewhat guilty he filed for custody of his boys and although he will never admit it, he is a little intimidated. Clarissa's tongue is as sharp as a two-edged sword when she's angry, and sometimes even when she's not. Plus he knows, like everyone else knows, family court is skewed in favor of mothers. Fathers seldom win.

Matthew's attorney has assured him he has a solid case, especially with the fact Clarissa takes her boys around her ex-con boyfriend. She thinks he doesn't know about that. To further strengthen his case, his attorney explained, Clarissa has alienated him from visiting with the boys and at least a couple of nights a week leaves them alone while she makes midnight rendezvous to her lover's house. She verbally abuses them when she doesn't get her way or they exert any amount of independence.

The boys deserve more.

Matt still finds it odd Clarissa has filed for adoption of her nephew, Tiger. In the fifteen years he's known Clarissa, he's never heard her mention his name and he's seldom heard her mention Tiger's mother Breanna. It's hard for Matt. On the whole he believes Clarissa is a good person and in his deepest heart, he wishes she could heal from her childhood trauma so that it wouldn't keep spilling over into her adult life. He believes everybody would be better for it, including and most importantly, his boys.

He's a little nervous about the upcoming hearing. His nervousness ceases as he finds out Clarissa's attorney filed a last minute motion for a continuance and for some unknown reason, the Judge grants the request.

CHAPTER 14
Sonya
July 2016

S onya gets into her tan Mercedes two-seater and opens the white leather top for fresh air. The brief wind blows her hair into her face. She pulls a few strands behind her ear and turns on the radio. Sonya's favorite song is playing. The sun spotlights her skin. Sonya knows she's gorgeous. She just wishes she felt gorgeous in the inside. She can't stop thinking about Thomas. She sure he's knows something; she's just not sure what. He's been more quiet than usual and that scares her or maybe it excites her, she's not sure. And then there's Tiger. Sonya thinks she has grown to love Tiger and very much wants to adopt him. She now loves nothing more than when he calls her "Mom." It makes her feel like she's done a good job. Sonya empathizes with Tiger never really having a mom, heck she never really did either. She relates to how painful it can be. Sonya accepts the stabilizing role she's playing in his life. In some sort of weird way, it helps her redeem the void in her own. Sonya has trouble understanding how anybody could ever give up such a precious soul, hers or Tiger's. Sonya has doubts lately. Not about the adoption, but about her marriage and is the adoption really a task she should be taking on now.

Sonya, parks at her favorite restaurant, Vine, where she's meeting four of her girlfriends, members of the professional football "wives club" for their monthly noonday lunch. Women who marry professional football players, coaches, or athletes in general involuntarily enter the wives club. Sonya finds resisting futile. She typically doesn't look forward to lunch, or to putting on airs, as most of the talk is usually caddy and materialistic. But, today, Sonya welcomes the diversion. The kids are in YMCA summer camp and Chloe is at doggie day care. She doesn't want to sit at home alone or risk the chance of running into Thomas between practices.

Two business men stop talking and stare as Sonya walks into the restaurant in her hot red fitted, sleeveless knee length cotton dress. She takes off her denim jacket revealing her lean, yet well sculpted arms. Her three gym memberships serve Sonya well. A man sitting at a corner table, drops his fork on the ground, excuses himself then retrieves it. Sonya is used to mesmerizing men, so she is unfazed.

Becky, the wife of one of the Bears' Receivers, points to the seat she saved for Sonya.

Becky's apple red and black print maxi dress drapes her ankles. Her long, lean model frame cuts ten years off her age.

Brenda and Jodi invite Sonya into the conversation. "Did you see what Toi posted yesterday?" "No," Sonya responds. *Nor do I care.*

A half an hour into lunch, Sonya grows tired of hearing about everyone's business while at the same time dodging questions about her own. She stares in the direction of the door and sees Harold Stone enter the restaurant with his wife. Sonya is ill at ease.

Becky seems to notice Sonya's discomfort, "How are the kids, Sonya?" she asks. It seems to Sonya that Becky always has it together. She's a career corporate attorney and has a solid marriage and unbelievably well-behaved children. Sonya often finds herself wishing for Becky's life. She wonders whether she would be cheating on her husband if she had what Becky has.

"Sonya, you're not eating your food," Becky notices, "Are you okay?"

Looking down at her plate, Sonya places the last bite of her grilled shrimp and mixed greens salad into her mouth and slowly looks up, "Yes-yes, I'm okay." She senses Becky is not convinced. Becky places a reassuring hand on Sonya's shaking knee under the table. Sonya looks up and stares directly into Becky's eyes, "I'm really okay." She knows Becky doesn't buy it.

After lunch, Sonya pulls Becky to the side and explains she really is okay. Becky looks directly into Sonya's eyes, maybe through her eyes and into her soul, "If you say so."

* * *

Thomas
That Same Day

The building is old, unassuming, and mostly weathered. Light yellow and gray bricks frame the private investigator's office building. Thomas climbs the four hard concrete steps and opens the door. It squeaks. Suite 333. Thomas looks down at the business card to make sure he has the right suite for Greg Story; former FBI agent turned private investigator. The halls smell like mildewed carpet which Thomas can barely see because the lights are dim, a stark contrast to the bright light outside.

Thomas still isn't sure he needs to take things this far. His best friend, Rob, the only person Thomas has confided his suspicions in, assured him he should at least take the in-person consult, and see what scoop Greg has already found from the phone consult Rob had with the assistant a couple of days prior. "After all," Rob reasoned, "it might all come out in the adoption. Better know now, then know later."

Thomas carefully opens the door to Greg's office suite. He feels like a ten-year-old child sneaking a cigarette in his back yard while his parents are at work. Thomas rubs his sweaty hands across his temples. "Hello," the middle-aged receptionist greets, "Please be seated. Greg will be with you momentarily," she continues. Thomas takes a seat on the worn couch from what has to be the seventies. He taps his foot. The suite is no more than a thousand square feet and consists of a receptionist area, a small conference room and the office of famously incognito, Greg Story. Thomas feels like he's in some sort of episode of "The Unit." He stares at all the clippings on the wall. To the side of Greg's office door is an 8x10 picture of a medium sized, average looking, African American woman shaking President Obama's hand. Directly under, is a picture of the same lady with the junior President Bush. Thomas begins to wonder is Greg a woman. Rob did all the preliminary work for him and left this fact out. Not that it matters.

"She's ready for you, Mr. Newman," says the receptionist.

Greg Story, short, totally unassuming woman, extends her hand and invites Thomas into her office. If Thomas had seen her on the street, he wouldn't have remembered a moment later.

After explaining the scope and pricing structure for Greg's services, she pauses and asks Thomas, "Mr. Newman, what is it you hope to find?"

"Nothin, I-I-I hope," he says.

His eyes well up with water. He looks away. Thomas fights to ensure no tears drop in Greg's presence. He moves to the edge of his seat. "I-I hope she's not cheating,"

Greg nods her head in understanding.

"What will you do if she is?"

Greg's receptionist buzzes in, "Greg, your daughter is on the line; she says it's urgent." Greg excuses herself and departs the office for what seems like a year. She returns.

"Greg," says Thomas, "I just need to know. One way or another, I need to know. I'll, I'll figure out what to do after that."

A small voice inside Thomas tells him he's about to be made a fool. He decides being a fool is light weight compared to the chronic agony he's been experiencing.

"Before we go further, Thomas says, "I want to make sure everything is confidential."

Greg responds, "Yes, as a matter of fact it is. As my assistant discussed with your friend during the previous half hour phone consult, I am bound by my license and industry standards to keep our work private except in limited circumstances, like a court order, but even then, I would offer only the minimal required."

Greg hopes no court will need this information.

"Mr. Newman, I know this is a delicate issue," Greg says. She pulls out a large white envelope from her file cabinet and drops in on her desk. "It's up to you whether we move forward or not. We can end it here if you'd like and pretend like nothing ever happened, or..."

"Actually, I am pretty sure she's cheating," Thomas blurts.

"Very well," says Greg. "I've done a little work since our first phone call.

She opens the envelope and pulls out four 8x12 pictures of Sonya and Bank of Braxton

President Harold Stone holding hands, kissing or otherwise touching one another.

"How-how can I make sure those pictures aren't Photoshopped?" says Thomas.

"We have no incentive to Photoshop, Mr. Newman. Furthermore, we use the most advanced recording and camera equipment that exists," she explains. "I can cover all original digital footage with you if you like Mr. Newman. I use multiple investigators and a diverse vehicle supply at any given time. All my investigators have served on local or state police forces, some the FBI, like myself, and most have been expert court witnesses. Authentication is the least of our concerns."

Thomas is silent.

"I don't doubt your capabilities. This is just a little mindboggling," says Thomas. He grabs his head to see if he can stop it from spinning. He begins to feel nauseous.

"I understand. It's very sensitive stuff, Mr. Newman." She coughs and says, "Have you ever considered counseling...he or she may help you decide how to go forward."

"No, counseling is for crazy people," Thomas replies.

He pauses, "just because my wife may be cheating, doesn't mean I'm crazy."

"Point well taken," nods Greg.

Thomas calls Sonya and the phone goes straight to voicemail, which is full.

CHAPTER 15
The Battle: Matthew and Clarissa
Braxton City County Building, Superior Court,
Family Division
July 2016

Matthew runs into Clarissa in the weathered hallway right outside a row of six court rooms. The City County building was built in 1965 and has had few renovations since then. Two wings, East and West were added to the twenty-six floor center tower in the 1980s. Matthew takes an emotional walk down memory lane as he proceeds through the east wing security check point. He places his belt back through his gray-blue dress pant loops and for a brief moment, sudden warmth fills his heart. Matthew remembers going through the same checkpoint as a little boy on his weekly visits to see his grandfather, the Honorable Patrick Chavis. He proceeds to the elevator.

In the hallway, Clarissa notices Matthew's head to toe suit and tie and reaches for her brown sweater jacket covering the top of her black straight-legged jeans and zips it up. Clarissa knows how to dress for court, but mostly prides herself in bucking formalities. Today is one of those days. She figures judges side with mothers most of the time anyway, so why impress. They enter the courtroom.

A few minutes later, after everyone is seated, the court bailiff calls the Moore custody case and the Judge swears in all parties. The court proceeding begins.

It's Clarissa's turn to take the witness stand.

"Ms. Moore," Matthew's attorney says, "Please state and spell your first and last name for the record." Clarissa obliges.

"Do you understand why we are here today?" she asks.

"Yes," says Clarissa.

"Why are we here?" the attorney asks.

"For Matthew's custody request," Clarissa responds.

"You've filed contempt for support on Matthew, is that not correct?" Matthew's attorney asks.

"Yes, he owes me."

"What does he owe you?"

"Summer academic enrichment programs, school loan fees for when I was in college, tutoring for the boys, football camp fees and a lot of other stuff. You have the documents, don't you? Why are you asking me?"

"Ms. Moore, what year are we in?"

"2016."

"I've looked through your motion for contempt and most of the expenses you've stated go back to 2004. Is there a reason?"

Clarissa rolls her eyes, "No."

"What year were you divorced?"

"2006."

"Do you find it odd your contempt filing was made one week after Matthew filed for primary custody?"

Clarissa purses her lips to the left of her mouth and rolls her neck to the side. "No."

"Yea okay," the attorney says loudly under her breathe.

"Moving on to the braces expense you are requesting reimbursement for; what makes you think Matthew is responsible?"

"Because he's their father."

"Okay," says the lawyer, "Let's talk more about the braces. How old are your children?"

"Jeremy is 10 and Joey is 12," Clarissa responds."

The judge looks up from the legal pad she was using to take notes.

Matthew softly clears his throat.

"Ms. Moore, did you consult with Matthew before you obtained braces?

"No, I don't have to. It was phase 1 of the plan."

"Did you obtain a second orthodontic opinion before you secured braces?"

"No?" responds Clarissa, "I don't have to. I'm the mother and I know what I'm doing."

"And Mr. Newman is to pay for you knowing what you are doing?"

"Your Honor, that's not a question," demands Clarissa's attorney.

Clarissa stares at the Matthew's attorney through half-cocked eyes and taps her tennis shoe.

She places her once raised hand down on the hard wood arm of the cold witness stand. A tear drops from her eye.

"Ms. Moore, what type of custody do you currently have?"

"Full custody, my children are with me," she answers.

"No ma'am, will you please read the fifth paragraph of your divorce settlement I've set before you?"

Clarissa pulls out her reading glasses, "While mother maintains sole physical custody, parties shall have joint legal custody and shall make decisions relating to education, religion, health and any other major issues jointly."

"Okay," says the attorney, "Will you please skip down to paragraph seven and read aloud?"

Clarissa complies, "Mother shall notify father by email within 30 days of a desired expenditure and father will respond by email within two weeks regarding whether he agrees to said expenditure. Once agreement is reached, mother will be responsible for 30% of said expenditure and father will be responsible for 70%."

Clarissa looks up from her readers and blurts, "Well then he's responsible for 70%."

The judge looks up. The court reporter stops typing.

"And the agreement, Ms. Moore?" questions the attorney.

Clarissa, in elevated voice says, "I thought we were here for custody."

"I did too," says the attorney, "until you filed a support contempt alleging Matthew owes you money. So let's keep talking."

"It's my understanding the children will need braces again," says the attorney, "when they're older and you're asking this cost be covered, too?"

Clarissa slouches in her seat and stares straight ahead. She nods her head up and down.

The attorney continues, "Do you think maybe had you consulted with Matthew beforehand, he may have objected to the children having braces so early? And that maybe, just maybe you made a costly snap decision?"

"I can't say," says Clarissa

"My point exactly," responds the attorney.

"Moving on to custody, are you aware the Domestic Evaluator takes issue with your new boyfriend and his background?"

"No, I haven't read the report."

Clarissa's attorney looks away.

"Where do you think the best place for two growing boys is, with their mother or with their father? You've already proved it can't be both."

"Objection," shouts Clarissa's attorney.

"Withdrawn," responds Matthew's attorney.

He continues, "Ms. Moore, you're receiving alimony, correct?"

"You tell me," Clarissa responds.

"I'll take that as a yes. Your honor, will you please let the record reflect?"

"So ordered," commands Judge Chavis. He motions for Matthew's attorney to continue.

"How much alimony and child support are you receiving?"

Clarissa responds.

The attorney continues, "I understand you are in an adoption battle with Bears Quarterback, Thomas Newman over his foster child," says the lawyer.

"He's my nephew," Clarissa snaps.

"Have you met him?"

"I object," interrupts Clarissa's attorney, "Relevance?"

"Sustained," says Judge Chavis.

"Are you receiving a monthly payment for his adoption?"

"I haven't heard," answers Clarissa.

"Is there a possibility for you to receive federal money if the Adoption Court grants your adoption?"

"Possibly, I heard about something, but I'm not sure."

"No further questions.

Matthew takes the stand.

Clarissa's attorney combines cross examination and direct examination.

"Mr. Moore, you didn't pay for braces did you?"

"No, I had no idea the boys needed them and was only told about them after the orthodontist put them on. I went to the office where they got them and learned they truly were optional." Matthew responds.

After four or five similar questions, the attorney asks the judge to accept a summary statement she created to support finding

Matthew is in contempt of his child support.

Matthew's attorney does not object.

"Any more testimony?" Judge Chavis asks.

"We rest," says Matthew's attorney.

Judge Chavis looks at Clarissa's lawyer.

"We rest."

"Please submit your proposed findings of fact and proposed orders within the next two weeks. I will mail my decision to counsel," directs Judge Chavis.

He stands, "All rise," says the bailiff.

Matthew, Clarissa and their attorneys stand. Judge Chavis exits.

Within a week, both Clarissa's attorney and Matthew's attorney submit ten page documents explaining to the Judge why he should rule in their favor.

The Judge deliberates independently in his office and sends his final order. Clarissa's attorney delivers the bad news, she lost custody of the boys and Judge Chavis denied her contempt petition.

CHAPTER 16
Clarissa
July 2016

Clarissa sits in the passenger seat of her uncle's red Ford pick-up. It's a hot eighty-seven degrees in Braxton with a few clouds sprinkled above. The buckle clicks as Clarissa fastens her belt. New car smell permeates the air. Clarissa is looking forward to the four and a half hour drive to Cartersville, Virginia with Uncle Charlie to celebrate the life and death of her favorite singing legend, Turner Stevens. Turner was more than a singer; he was a hall of fame activist for the rights of all people – no matter the race, religion, sexual preference, identity or ethnicity.

Uncle Charlie is still the only family member on Clarissa's dad's side she keeps up with. He places his huge, paternal right hand on top of Clarissa's delicate left shoulder and steers the gigantic leather wheel. "Hang in there, Clara. This too shall pass."

Clarissa reclines her tan leather seat and places her bare feet onto her uncle's dashboard. Uncle Charlie turns toward Clarissa and grins with satisfaction.

After a few moments of silence, Uncle Charlie looks her direction, "Clara, have you been going to church?"

"No, Unc, and to be quite truthful, I'm really not sure I believe in God anymore."

Uncle Charlie stares ahead.

He turns his satellite radio to a jazz station and for the next couple of hours, they groove to chaotic rhythm.

Clarissa and Uncle Charlie arrive at the Cartersville amphitheater two hours earlier than the program's start. Clarissa is in awe of the extent and expense to which the Stevens family indulged; all to put together such a meaningful program - open to the general public. Upon entering the theater, Clarissa is handed a black, silver and gold textured program. The back reads:

"Everything you experience today has the blessing of our loving brother Turner. It is with his detailed planning prior to his death, this program was created in his honor and in to celebrate his greatness. Thank you."

They find their seats and Clarissa leaves for the ladies room.

The closer Clarissa gets to the bathroom, the more people she sees flooding into the amphitheater. Women wearing bright red, green, gold color floor length dresses and men wearing black beanies capture her attention on her return.

I can't believe I'm actually here.

Clarissa has loved Turner since she was a little girl and remembers listening to his music on Saturday mornings at her uncle's house.

Clarissa smells something cooking. She moves towards the scent and discovers mini roast beef and smoked turkey sandwiches on several long rectangular tables provided by the Stevens family. A life size black and white picture of Turner displays on the upper wall between the two tables. Clarissa grabs several sandwiches, two containers of potato salad, napkins and plastic utensils for her and Uncle Charlie and heads back to her seat.

Clarissa smiles at Uncle Charlie as she

approaches and excuses herself while she steps in front of a gorgeous, blonde German lady seated next to him. Clarissa sits to his left. At that moment, the most beautiful person Clarissa has ever seen, a Somali woman, dressed in a royal blue robe trimmed in bright yellow and matching hijab covering her head, delicately seats herself at Clarissa's right. Joined by the lady are friends dressed in bright orange, green, and gold robes, one wearing a hijab and the other without. Clarissa hears the clanging of the women's silver and gold bracelet bangles decorating the entirety of their arms as they sweetly chatter in an unknown dialect.

"Check one, check two," says the sound guy, "I think we've got it, Sam," he continues. The bright concert lights over the distant stage flip on.

Like a child experiencing life for the first time, Clarissa turns to her Uncle Charlie and says "This is amazing Unc. Thanks again for inviting me." Uncle Charlie gives a reassuring smile.

Clarissa sits back in her seat - it squeaks. The air conditioner is roaring. She sneezes and unknots her white sweater from her waist, drapes it around her shoulders, and puts her head on her uncle's shoulder.

Later, all but the stage lights slowly turn down and three life size video screens surrounding the stage flicker on. A charming young French Priest extends a welcome in his native language to the now over capacity sized crowd. Although there is no translator, Clarissa understands the spirit of the welcome.

Next, a Jewish Rabbi walks to the podium and says "We are all but one race, human." The crowd roars. The Rabbi proceeds to recount how Turner once asked him to join him for a tee time at a local golf course Turner had frequented for years. Turner explained the Club had always been kind to him and didn't make a fuss about him being an African American. Before saying yes, the Rabbi asked Turner the name of the club. Once Turner told him, he informed Turner that specific golf club was "restricted." Turner asked the Rabbi what he meant by "restricted." The Rabbi went on to explain "restricted" means Jewish people were not allowed. Turner never went to the club again. A powerful stillness permeates the air.

A charismatic Baptist preacher approaches the podium and Clarissa and Uncle Charlie scoot to the edge of their seat. He recounts how Turner's decision to face-off a national white supremacist organization inspired him as a young boy to hold on to his own convictions. "Because of his example, I am the man I am."

Clarissa considers herself Baptist and was once an avid church goer. Not only has she grown tired of capital campaigns, incessant sermons on tithing, and one affair after another between church members and the pastors; but she just doesn't know how she feels about God anymore. *How can a God who is so loving allow so much pain? Why did I never receive nurturing from my mother and father? Why did I lose my sons? Will I lose Tiger?*

Clarissa softly cries. She thinks no one can hear her. A Buddhist man behind her taps her shoulder and hands her his handkerchief.

The Center stage screen flickers off and turns on again just as a Native American Faithkeeper, in full tribal garment recounts how Turner Stevens supports Indigenous people. He goes on to tell how he marched with Native Americans during the "Lengthiest Walk" to Washington.

"Turner, Turner, Turner," the crowd roars. Uncle Charlie leans back in his chair in satisfaction. He turns to Clarissa, "The four hour trip was worth it, eh?"

Clarissa nods her head yes. "And even the four hour trip back home," she grins.

Just then, Clarissa notices an old boyfriend seated a row in front of her. She taps him on the shoulder, "Hello, Al." Al turns around and smiles. He introduces Clarissa to his wife sitting beside him. "Nice to meet you," she says.

Al is the one that got away. Clarissa would give anything to go back in time. She would have done things differently. Life was simpler then, no children, and no stresses. Al respected her, truly loved her. Clarissa is beginning to realize now that she didn't, and maybe still doesn't, know how to receive true love from a mate. *Yes, he's the one that got away.*

Two Buddhist monks, barefoot and draped in orange and yellow robes, catch

119

Clarissa's attention on center stage as they chant mantras to a unique drum beat.

"I'm mesmerized." Clarissa says as she turns to Uncle Charlie.

Unc winks, "Me too."

Clarissa doesn't want the service to end, but it does and she and Uncle Charlie head to the truck.

On their drive back to Braxton, Clarissa can tell Uncle Charlie wants to talk about more than the funeral services.

"What about you my love?" he finally asks.

A tear drops from her eye.

"I'm in pain, Unc and some days I don't know if I can make it," she says.

I know you don't see it now, Clara," says Uncle Charlie, "but there's always a purpose. I know losing the boys hurts you, and going through your divorce still hurts you. Please know that seasons change and that this pain, too, shall pass. It just does, Clara. I'm a living witness."

Clarissa shifts in her seat and Uncle Charlie digs in further. "Sometimes, God allows pain, Clara, not only for us to see who He is, but to refine our character. Some of our best learning comes in the midst of a valley. Some of our best character development can only be accomplished through pain. Let the pain do what it is purposed to do. Let it make you, Clara."

Flashes of her father beating her mother when she was three and of her brother making her grab pennies from piping hot water come and leave Clarissa's mind. She balls in a fetal position against the passenger door and wails. She rocks to self soothe and eventually catches her breath.

Uncle Charlie, typically a man of few words with a big heart, grabs her hand.

Clarissa wonders if her problems with men stem from the disrespect and outright abuse she not only witnessed as a child, but experienced herself from almost every important man in her life; every man except Uncle Charlie, Matthew and Al. She reflects on the twenty-one-year-old cousin who, when she was twelve, took her to an Olympic viewing party with his college friends and raped her right after. She had admired her cousin and was regrettably smitten by his whispered grooming compliments about how mature she was and how her body looked like most of the college girls he knew. She remembers him firing up a joint and blowing the smoke into her mouth as he kissed her. For years, Clarissa has pushed this memory out of her head, but for some reason today, she knows she needs to come to grips with it. She doesn't dare tell her Uncle. He's saved and all, but an ass whooping he will grant to anyone hurting his Clara.

Clarissa slams her head into her lap and cries out loud for long moments while Uncle Charlie keeps his loving hand on her back.

"I don't know all of it, Clara, but I know some of it," he eventually says. "Let it all out, my precious baby girl. Let it out."

Grabbing inner strength, Clarissa is able to regain composure and looks up, "Thank you for loving me."

CHAPTER 17
Thomas
July 2016

Thomas leaves Greg's office impaired by the black smoke and tar emitting from all four wheels of his Porsche. Rolling ninety-five miles per hour on the Braxton freeway, he narrowly misses a dog darting across the highway. He pulls over in the bank's parking lot. Harold's car is gone, so he heads home. Thomas has never missed a football meeting in his seven years as the Bears Quarterback. There's a first for everything.

Thomas calls Sonya again. No answer.

Why? How? When? How Long?

Thomas swerves into the middle lane. An oncoming car honks three times and its driver flips Thomas the bird. He swerves back into the fast lane. Thomas sees a cop ahead and drops his speed down to seventy-five. Lucky for him, the officer pulls over the car directly in front of him. Thomas slows down.

Uninvited thoughts infiltrate his head. All the phone calls, the claims that her mother was sick, her unexplained departures. It all makes sense. Thomas flashed backed to his childhood when his mother found out his dad had been cheating on her for years with the neighbor. He recalled how much the lady's boy looked like Thomas and his sister. The pain punched quicker and harder than a professional boxer's uppercut.

Thomas wishes he had someone to really talk to. On the other hand, he doesn't want anyone other than Rob to know. Rob is not the deep, mushy kind of guy and would probably encourage Thomas to whoop Sonya's ass. He grew up around violence, so while he's a good man, that's what he knows. Rob's not the person to talk to right now.

Thomas gets an untimely call from his favorite receiver, EJ. He quickly contemplates telling E.J what's going on, but is interrupted by EJ's teary sobs. EJ tells Thomas his niece was just found dead in her dorm room. She was a star freshman basketball player at the

Braxton University. No foul play was suspected and reports say she hung herself. EJ's niece had struggled every since she was kicked out of her parent's home for admitting to them she was gay. She lived with EJ and his wife throughout her last two years of high school.

Thomas subconsciously welcomes the diversion.

Thomas pulls into his driveway and opens the garage door. He doesn't see Sonya's car. He's furious. The kids are with their grandmother. He heads to his downtown guest penthouse. He suspects Sonya has used it a time or two.

The entrance is brightly lit and George, the doorman, opens the door.

"Hello, Mr. Newman," he says nervously.

Thomas checks his pockets and finds a pack of gum, but can't find his key. The Concierge smiles and gives him a replacement. "We haven't seen you in a while."

Thomas manages a smile.

A bell rings and the red light for the thirty-first floor lights up above Thomas's head. Thomas gets off the elevator.

Thomas hovers his key over the keypad. The green light appears. He thinks he hears a noise, but is not sure. Calling the police is not an option. Thomas's testosterone is pumping. He's got this. He opens the cabinet containing his handgun and grabs it. He hears a lamp fall, but is unsure whether it is in his unit or the unit next door. Whispering fills the air. No, this is definitely his unit.

He hears a man's voice. It's familiar. Thomas wonders if he has walked in on the middle of a robbery and takes his gun off safety. Thomas hears a female whisper. He wonders is this the maid and what kind of shenanigans are really going on.

Then, there's a moan, a groan and a laugh.

He opens the bedroom door and sees none other than his wife Sonya on top of a muscular cherry black man with her legs straddling his waist. Sonya turns her head. Her mouth drops. Thomas lunges at Sonya and Harold and inadvertently drops his gun.

Freshly cut chocolate dipped pineapples and strawberries fall on the floor knocking over a lit candle. A fire ignites.

"Aaaaaah shit," says Harold.

Thomas reaches for Harold's neck.

Harold grabs his pants and heads for the door.

Thomas finds his gun and fires two shot. The second hits Harold on his thoroughbred like hamstring.

A neighbor must have heard the commotion because the police arrive moments later. The officers arrest Thomas.

CHAPTER 18
Braxton County Jail, Thomas
Two Days later

A deafening buzz followed by large hollow booted footsteps move in Thomas's direction. Thomas takes his last piss in the miniature jail cell toilet that has housed him for the last forty-eight hours. A little pee splatters on the cold concrete floor and drips down the crusted drain. The steel bars slowly open and the guard cuffs Thomas's hands behind his sky blue county jump suit. "Braxton DOC," in broken tan stencil, decorates his now bowed shoulders. "Mr. Newman, follow me," says the Corrections Officer in a deep voice.

Relieved, yet bothered, Thomas surveys the uniformed man's pale brown, army like pants decorated at the waist by sparkling handcuffs, radio, baton, flashlight, Taser, and firearm. Thomas can't keep his eyes off the officer's fire arm, all twenty-four inches of readymade projectile. The officer grabs Thomas's left shoulder and directs him forward. The front desk guard throws Thomas's personal belongings into a clear trash bag and bids him farewell. Thomas signs the papers the guard puts in front of him and exits. The officer unlocks his cuffs and Thomas looks at the small card now in his hands. His pre-trial hearing for attempted manslaughter is set for September 22, 2016.

Rob waits in a vehicle just outside the jail's gate. Thomas, reassured he can always count on the brother he never had, jumps in the car. The sun seems brighter, the air fresher and the birds are certainly chirping louder. Yes, louder - at least for a moment.

Before driving out of the jail's heavily guarded rear employee's entrance; a nerdy curly haired wiring-glasses-sporting twenty-something darts in front of Rob's car with microphone in hand. The news reporter is followed by his camera man who's followed by three officers. "Did you do it, Mr. Newman? Did you shoot Harold Stone?" he shouts.

Rob looks at Thomas in the passenger seat. "Twenty points," he says jokingly. Thomas manages a slight grin. He's not feeling humorous, but knows Rob is trying to lighten the mood. Rob knows Thomas would never consent to him hitting a reporter with his car for "twenty points." But if it accidentally happens...

Unsure whether Rob can successfully dodge the rushing sea of cameras and reporters, he's relieved Rob somehow does just that.

"Mr. Newman, is your wife having an affair?" one asks as Rob's car rolls by. Rob almost accidentally runs over the reporter's foot.

"What about Tiger's adoption? What does Tiger think about this?" yells another. Rob speeds up and pulls the car outside the entrance.

He pushes a hundred miles per hour on highway 33 and passes a blue uniformed police officer waiving a neon orange flashing stick directing them to exit ahead. Rob obliges. Another officer motions for Rob to turn onto a deserted road. He does and then he pulls into a barren gas station. "Hello," says a third officer, "your car is waiting, Mr. Newman."

Thomas slowly extends his arm to shake the officer's hand, "Thank you."

"No problem, Mr. Newman, we protect all our citizens, no matter what." The officer reaches inside the window of his parked squad car pulls out a sharpie and a football. He motions for an autograph."

While Thomas is signing the ball, Rob slips the officer an envelope with ten crisp one hundred dollar bills.

Rob and Thomas drive away in a dark blue Chevrolet. They pull up to the backside entrance of the Avante, a boutique hotel frequented by elite VIPs, celebrities, and diplomats. After obtaining the key from the concierge's desk, Rob brings it to Thomas, and they proceed to the private suite.

Rob turns on the T.V.

"This is Caine Andrews from ESPN News. As you see Braxton Bears Quarterback great Thomas Newman has just posted bond and has been released from jail pending trial. He's been charged with attempted manslaughter in the shooting of Bank of Braxton President, Harold Stone. As you might expect, Mr. Newman is not answering questions from reporters. Details regarding the criminal trial are unfolding. So far, ESPN has learned a hearing has been set on an undisclosed date."

Thomas opens a beer before flopping onto the couch. He extends his hand in the air like he watches the black players on the team do before they engage in a soul shake. Rob has seen it too, so he reciprocates. Their hands smack in the air. "You always come through," says Thomas.

"You've got it brother," Rob responds.

Rob pulls out a marijuana joint and lights it up. Thomas uncharacteristically takes a hit. Most of Thomas's tension melts away.

Rob looks straight into Thomas's tired eyes, "Tommy, how are you holding up?" he asks.

Thomas is silent. And dazed.

"Not sure that I am," he finally responds.

Rob continues, "Man, I would never ask you if you did it or why. I just want you to know I will do all I can. I'm sticking right by your side."

Thomas sighs.

After Rob leaves, Thomas closes his eyes and is surprised he is able to sleep, maybe that's because he hasn't done so in what seems like weeks.

After waking up from a deep trance, Thomas turns on the midnight news. There's something inside that makes him want to see what people think, what they are saying. To his awkward surprise, he's not the hot topic of the late night. Instead, that sickbag USA junior boy's football coach, David Parona and his parole hearing are. Thomas listens to the reporters recount how Parona started the new league and how he used his power as a coach and director of his charity, "Raising Men", to groom fragile, mostly single-parent home, young men with gifts and trips to engage in sexual acts with them. Thomas is disgusted as he watches old news clips of Parona standing at a podium declaring his innocence with his wife by his side. Then, he wonders. He wonders if Tiger was ever one of Parona's victims. He did a short stint at "Raising Men."

Thomas misses Tiger. He misses TJ and

Dotty and Sonya, too. But there's something about Tiger. *I know he's scared. He's been through so much. I just can't imagine what's going on.*

CHAPTER 19
Tiger
July 2016

Tiger silently sits in Denise's car and quickly wipes the lonely tears filling his eyes. He screams and rams his shoulder into the passenger's door and reaches for the handle. Denise hits the safety lock just in time. He can't believe he has to leave the Newman family. He doesn't care what they're saying on television. His dad didn't do it.

"I know it doesn't seem like it will be ok, but trust me, Tiger, it will," says Denise. Tiger grows quiet - quiet and confused.

Why didn't they want me? "Did I do something wrong?" I must have done something wrong.

"Ms. Denise," Tiger finally murmurs as he looks ahead. Denise momentarily takes her eyes off the road and looks at Tiger in the passenger seat. "Yes." "Am I going to Mama

Paula's?" he asks.

Denise smiles, "You bet you are."

Tiger relaxes.

Although Denise doesn't usually mix placement transports, DCS is short staffed which leaves her with little choice. "Tiger, we're going to make one stop." Denise turns into the DCS office to pick-up a fourteen-year-old girl, Kya, who was dropped off by her father for cutting herself. She's been in the DCS system for one thing or another since she was six.

Tiger is excused to the all-purpose game room. The room is filled with bright blue, orange and red tables. Board games like Sorry and a Dominos game sit on each table. A flat screen television perches high on the back wall. Only two other children, both younger than Tiger, occupy the room. Tiger sits in a back corner, turns on the television and changes the channel to the sports station. He hopes to see his dad on television.

The girl is escorted by a policewoman to Denise. Kya walks slowly with her head to the ground. Two blue wrist bands cover old, healed cuts on her left arm; a white bandage is placed over her fresh wound on her right. She seats herself in a chair beside Denise.

Denise takes a quick look at her file summary sheet the officer hands her and learns a lot.

At the tender age of twelve, Kya was molested by an Internet predator. Posing as a fourteen-year-old boy, Kya's thirty-seven old perpetrator befriended her in the chat room, "School Daze." After convincing her she was the most beautiful "girl" in the world and that her parents were far too strict, he encouraged her to send him naked photos. Once he got the photos, he threatened to send them to her parents if she didn't do what he wanted her to do - which was to send more. The predator complimented Kya on her grown-up body. He asked her to stay home from school one day. She said yes. That day he raped her. In her investigative statement, Kya's interviewer said Kya "has felt raped every day since; especially, when she had to tell and retell her story to the cops, her parents, the Prosecutor and the Defense Attorney."

Denise puts down the summary. *The bastard had the nerve to hire a Defense Attorney.*

Digging further in the file, Denise comes across a report from a year prior. "To cope, Kya has started taking pills she's obtained from older school mates. She's run away from her father's home several times. It is suspected, she strips to support her habit."

Denise smiles at Kya. She looks towards the floor. Denise gently directs her down the hall to a vacant room. Offering Kya a seat, Denise looks her in the eye and asks "How are you?" Kya shrugs her shoulders. "Listen, Kya, I know it's tough." Denise scoots close. "Well, I don't know exactly how you feel." She touches Kya's knee. Kya manages a brief smile. Denise makes a few calls and lets Kya know she's going to take her to a local group home while she searches for more suitable placement.

Denise takes Kya to the group home and heads back to DCS to retrieve Tiger to take him to Mama Paula's. They remain silent during most of the forty-five minute drive.

As they pull into her driveway, Denise says, "Tiger, you'll just be here a little while until we can find you a more permanent placement," He opens his car door and jumps outside.

Mama Paula, in a pale pink knee length cotton dress, opens the metal screen door and greets Tiger with her usual jolly ear-to-ear smile. "Here are your towels and sheets, Sugar," she motions to Tiger. "Now, go on upstairs and wash up and make your bed," she says. He cheerfully grabs the sheets from Mama Paula's arms. She winks, "You know where it is."

Tiger smiles.

Tiger loves his room in Ms. Paula's house. He wonders if all of her foster kids feel like it's their room, too. The walls are painted dark taupe. The light brown carpet is fresh and spotless. The closet is filled with male clothes from toddler's size one to adult extra large. Figurines of baseball players, hockey players, and basketball and football players overfill the two dressers. The same green fern he remembers sprouts even bigger from a pot on the floor.

Tiger wonders if his real grandmother on his dad's side is like Mama Paula. His mom once told him his grandmother is a dark skinned African American woman with more love to give than the world could attempt to hold. He wonders if she even knows he exists. He's heard so many lies, Tiger wonders if she is even African American or if she really can give that kind of love - the kind of love he needs. He hears rumblings that he's mixed, and figures it's true because, even though he's pale as a white bucket in the winter, he tans to an awfully solid caramel in the warmer months. Tiger wishes he could have met his biological father before he was murdered. He's overheard his mother bragging to her family that Tiger's father would have been a big professional football star with at least a million dollars in the bank had he not gotten caught up with the wrong crowd. If only he could even see a picture of his father. No one seems to have one, or so they say. Does his mother even really know who his father is? Without a name, Tiger may just never know.

In fresh pajamas and smelling like Old Spice soap—his favorite—Tiger walks down the stairs and hugs Mama Paula around the waist. She hums old Christian hymnals as she rolls the dough for her infamous homemade buttermilk biscuits. The mouth-watering, warm smell of fresh bread slowly permeates the air. It sets Tiger more at ease. Mama Paula takes the piping hot biscuits out of the oven and drains the bacon and sausage she prepared on a nearby paper towel. "His eye is on the sparrow, I know He watches me…," she sings. Tiger feels right home, at peace, as if there is nowhere he is supposed to be. He sits down. Places his elbow onto the table and rests his head. Mama Paula places two fingers under his chin and tilts his face up so that his eyes directly meet hers, smiles and says, "This too shall pass, my son. It always does, and it always will." Ms. Denise, seated in a chair opposite Tiger, agrees.

Tiger hears a baby cry and spots a white crib in the corner of the kitchen he hadn't noticed before. Ms. Denise grabs the blue and white bib and hands it to Mama Paula who bottle feeds the three day old. The baby calms and gurgles. Tiger asks if he can hold her.

After a breakfast, Ms. Denise leaves, and Tiger climbs the stairs to takes a much-needed nap. Four hours later, he awakes. In "his room," Tiger feels safe. He enjoys the reliable warmth.

141

He asks Mama Paula, who is sitting in a nearby reclining chair knitting a baby blanket, "Where am I going?"

She pats the back of the baby resting on her lap under the yarn, "I'm not sure, Honey,"

Tiger goes outside and helps the caretaker feed the horses. He wonders how many kids like him they've seen.

The next morning, Tiger gets his answer. "Baby, I just got off the phone with Ms. Denise," Mama Paula says at breakfast. Looks like you're going to stay with your Aunt Clarissa," Tiger pounds his fist on the table. He's not happy.

* * *

Home of Clarissa
August 2016

The doorbell rings and Clarissa trips over the dog's favorite toy while scurrying to answer. The toy squeaks and the dog barks. Clarissa rubs her new hip bruise, still throbbing. *Pesky wooden desk corner.* Taking short, fast breathes, Clarissa opens door.

Freshly baked double chocolate chip cookies and homemade meatballs and spaghetti fill the air. Clarissa watches Tiger twitch his nose in approval. Grabbing the tray of cookies placed on the table to the right of the door, Clarissa extends the multi-color rectangular cookie tray to Tiger. He grabs a cookie, looks up and grabs another with his other hand.

Placing her first three fingers and thumb on Tigers right shoulder, Denise gently encourages Tiger to go further into the house. "It's not what you're used to," Clarissa says. Tiger shrugs his shoulders and looks away.

Denise says, "Tiger, this is your aunt, Clarissa. She's your mother's sister." Tiger looks up slightly. "You're going to be staying here," Denise explains.

Tiger drops his black, over sized duffle bag on the entry way floor.

Clarissa reaches out for his hand. Tiger retracts, resolutely staring at the ground. Tears build in his eyes, and then rhythmically drop to the ground. Denise hugs him while he sobs. He holds on to her tightly and buries his head between her breast and arm pit. He whimpers. Denise holds Tiger tighter and rocks him side to side.

Clarissa remembers tips she was given at her recent kinship foster care training. She pulls up a chair, but not too close. She tries everything she knows to try, but Tiger still will not talk to Clarissa. Clarissa was used to commanding her boys to talk when they didn't feel like it. A myriad of thoughts compete in her mind: *Now, why am I doing this? He doesn't like me. He's scared. This little boy is going to have to learn how to shape up.* When she begins to feel hopeless, Clarissa remembers she's already set an appointment for Tiger to meet with her therapist tomorrow. Clarissa has been seeing her therapist every since her trip with Uncle Charlie. She was resistant at first, but every session is easier and easier. There's something about venting to someone who is skilled at empathy that she really enjoys. Slowly, but surely, Clarissa believes she's healing. Clarissa is working through her pain from her custody loss of the boys and more importantly she's beginning to identify that her real pain comes not from her ex husband, but from the abandonment of her father and her mother's inability to nurture her as a child—or ever. Clarissa is beginning to understand how all of her unresolved pain is manifesting itself in her life today and is dedicated to work towards changing that.

Although she recognizes she is a work in process and change will not come easily, she is starting to realize the filters she uses when perceiving something done "to her" are actually malfunctioning because she is deeply wounded. Her reactions to Matthew, his new wife, teachers at school when she doesn't get her way, and even her boys really have very little to do with the people themselves. Subconsciously, she sees her mother and father in every one of them and Clarissa is tired. She is learning that because of her unresolved trauma, she has perpetually re-created chaos in her life and she wants to do better. She knows she's not a bad person but that a lot of the things she has done to people, however, have been bad and that they may or may not forgive her, but that she is going to work on herself, regardless. Dagger doesn't understand and says she's changed. She told him to take a hike.

145

Clarissa hopes Tiger will warm up to her and she believes she's up for the challenge of helping him sort through whatever needs to be sorted through.

Denise, Tiger and Clarissa eat the spaghetti and garlic bread dinner Clarissa prepared and Denise says her goodbyes. Tiger's tears return. A couple of minutes later, the doorbell rings.

"Hey, Mom!" Joey and Jeremy scream as they run and hug her.

Looking at Tiger, Jeremy asks "Is this him?"

Clarissa nods.

"He looks just like us," says Joey

Tiger lifts his hazel eyes in the direction of Joey's and notices Joey's eyes look just like his own. He's confused, angry and confused. Tiger rages inside, but doesn't understand why. Tiger doesn't know whether he's coming or going; who loves him, who doesn't; where he will be or how long. He slams his fist on his leg and clenches his teeth. Clarissa startles and regains her composure.

Clarissa is grateful Matthew lets the boys visit even more than their court order requires, but just wonders if Tiger can ever truly adjust to a life with them, a life with family he doesn't even know.

CHAPTER 20
Braxton DCS Office, Denise
August 2016

Denise sits in the staleness of her division manager's office. The windows and doors are closed. Denise feels closed. Case workers scurry to meet office imposed deadlines and cases continue to pile up beyond the unenforced state standards. Denise looks squarely in Rob's eyes, "Bio mother wants Tiger back. Are you kidding me!" she exclaims.

Rob slams the file on top of his plastic wood like desk and quickly nods his head. He turns his head to the side and lifts his dusty red uni-brow.

Rob reaches forward and hands a stack of documents to Denise, "You'll need to do a visit with Tiger's bio mom, Breanna ASAP," he says.

"Breanna's Public Defender is asking that

her visits be re-instated," he continues. Even though her rights have been terminated, she's appealing the decision, so we may be caught between a rock and a hard place."

Denise drops her pen and taps her leg, "On what basis?"

Denise knows finding Breanna will be difficult as she somehow can't find the original file with all her contact info, and that even if she could, Breanna is a drug addict who is most times homeless. According to Denise's memory, when she has a cell phone, it's a throw away. Denise vaguely remembers hearing something about Breanna cleaning up her act, which is great. But that doesn't help much. She's not even sure her Public Defender can consistently reach her.

"Do you have contact information for Breanna?" Rob asks Denise.

Just then, Denise hears a baby cry behind her. She stands up, "Is that Jody?" Both she and Rob look towards the door, "You bouncin' back, kind a quick," Denise says as she hugs her former cubby mate who is now on maternity leave. Rob chats for a short while; he sees the DCS computer technician and excuses himself to talk with him about his laptop. While Rob is away, Denise leans in to Jody and whispers, "I need some advice about a case I have, Tiger McKenney. You've heard of him, right?" Jody nods her head.

Jody parks the stroller and flips the brakes. The baby passes foul gas. "Weren't you assigned to one of Tiger's siblings at one time?"

"Yes," Jody responds. "Give me the scoop on Breanna," Denise says.

Just then, Robs re-enters his office. Jody winks at Denise and motions for Denise to call her later. Jody leaves and searches the file spread wide open over his desk. "Today, Denise." She peruses the file.

Denise goes back to her desk and pulls up the DCS policy on bio parent visitation and termination of parental rights which states:

> Once a parent who has abused or neglected a child fails to comply with court ordered services and the court involuntarily takes his or her parental rights and said mother

150

or father files an appeal, the
Department of Child Services is
under no obligation to, but
can request that the court re-
instate visitation. DCS should
do so and should do
everything it can do to
facilitate visits.

Denise is stressed and needs to take her
mind off of the case; so she opens her social
media page. She sees an uncharacteristic post
from a former DCS attorney:

(Long post alert) Something
unusual happened yesterday. I
took my car to a local repair
shop in the Southern part of
the state where a twenty year
old young Caucasian man was
filling in for his dad. I did the
routine check-in and he
wouldn't look me directly in
my eyes. I'm pretty sure he's
never seen a black woman, let
alone one with a laptop. Later,

he began to talk. He told me his dad had a motorcycle accident. I listened... they were going to get revenge on the guy who caused the accident and that he considers himself "Southern." He pointed outside, "You see that huge Confederate flag down the street?" I got a little nervous, but shook my head up and down. I waited and took a chance. I asked, "If my car broke down in front of the Confederate flag, how would that work out for me?" Looking directly into my eyes, he said, "As long as you ain't asking for reparations, you'll be ok..." I said, "ooookaaay" and changed the subject. He kept talking. I kept listening. He asked me if I knew what "mudding" was and I told him no. He explained he and his friends drive their trucks through mud at high speeds and sometimes the wheels fall off. He invited me outside to see some of the trucks. I went and actually enjoyed learning about mudding. Just when I thought it wouldn't come up again, "Remember what I was saying about reparations?" I sighed inside. The young man proceeded to tell me he was at a restaurant and "a black man was at the counter asking for discounted food and yelling the staff was racist." The young man tapped the guy on the shoulder and said, "Racist?... You ain't never gonna get no reparations up here....That was 200 years ago...can you tell me which them there ancestor that it was done to? If you can't, ain't no racist in here and you need to get to going..." He pointed to his gun. The young man proceeded to tell me about all the guns he owns and that Black Lives Matter is part of the Black Panthers. I sighed slightly aloud. After about an hour, I told him, his father would be proud of the job he is doing running the shop and that maybe he's getting him ready to take over the shop one day. The young man stood still and looked into my eyes, "No way, I don't wanna be in automotives..." I wrinkled my forehead, "What do you want to be?" He said, "A Police Officer..." AND THEREIN LIES THE PROBLEM!!!! I probably won't get to see my new friend again as my husband has FORBADE me to ever go the repair shop. ☺

Denise is floored. The post has over 340 likes in just thirty minutes, many of which were angry faces. Denise shows it to two of her cubicle neighbors, one Latina and one Caucasian. They end up in a lengthy one-hour discussion about the very real issue of ignorance and race in America. Denise went into social work to help change the world. Now she wonders if she really can make an impact. *Maybe I can have an impact on Tiger's world at least.*

She goes back to her desk and opens her two-day-old chicken salad sandwich. She sifts through Tiger's file again and finds a wrinkled piece of paper with a lone phone number. Denise decides to take a chance and call the number.

The phone rings and Denise taps her pen on her desk. No one answers, and there's no opportunity to leave a message.

Denise asks a co-worker her opinion on Tiger's case. She has none.

She knocks on the door of the DCS attorney assigned to Tiger's case.

As she enters her office, Denise flashes back to how tightly Tiger held her when she dropped him off at Clarissa's. She's not sure at this point whether Tiger should be with

Breanna, Clarissa, or Thomas and Sonya.

Back at her desk, Denise places her ear buds in and turns on her favorite country artist. She does another fine tooth review of Tiger's file to see if she can learn any more about Tiger's biological mother. Breanna McKenney is a bi-racial female who had her first child as a teenager. She's been arrested for drug possession, possession of drug paraphernalia, prostitution - three times- and petty theft. She's maintained over ten noted places of residence and seems to changed her cell phone every thirty days or so. Two of Breanna's children were stillborn and most live births were born with some drug in their system.

Denise looks up Breanna's last known address and is not surprised to find out it's in the most drug infested projects in Braxton. The last visit Denise made to Breanna a year earlier left Denise fighting off dreams of roaches and dog feces. Denise remembers it like it was yesterday. She had facilitated a supervised visit between Tiger and Breanna at her downtown apartment. Breanna had been engaging in her court ordered services, so it appeared Breanna was really pulling things together. Tiger sat on the couch swatting roaches as they ran across his legs. Old and new dog feces overpowered Breanna's peach flavored Glad plug-ins. When Denise turned her head, she could have sworn Breanna pinched Tiger. He never admitted it one way or another and she couldn't know for sure. Breanna's speech was all over the place. Denise decided to do an on-site drug test and sure enough Breanna tested for low levels of about every drug known to man. As Denise grabbed Tiger to leave the visit, she heard gunshots in the backyard common area of the apartment and had to call the police department for assistance.

Denise picks up the wrinkled paper with mystery number and calls it again.

"Hello," someone says. "Is…is this Breanna?" asks Denise. "Yea," the voice says. Denise hears loud music blasting in the background, which she finds odd because it is in the middle of the day. She hears two men laughing. Denise draws her cup of overly sweetened coffee to her mouth.

Denise clears her throat, "I'm calling

about your son, Tiger. I understand you would like to see him."

Breanna breathes hard, "More than anything."

"Are you in a good position to see him, Breanna? Have you gained any stability?"

"I really have, Ms. Denise, and I got a job and a place to stay," says Breanna.

"You did?" asks Denise

"Yep, I work part time at the KFC," Breanna says.

"How long have you been there?" asks Denise.

"Two," says Breanna.

"Two what?" says Denise.

"Two months. Buuuut before there, I was at the Target and before then..." Breanna explains.

"I get it," Denise interrupts.

Denise takes another sip of coffee.

Although Denise fundamentally believes every child should be with his or her biological parent if possible, she's not so sure she can support Tiger being in the care of his mother. She hopes something works out, but just doesn't know.

"Let's talk more when I come and see you," Denise says to Breanna.

"Is Tiger coming?" Breanna asks. *In your dreams*, Denise wants to say. "No, not this time, but maybe next time," Denise responds. "Who do you live with?" Denise asks Breanna.

The phone disconnects. Denise looks down at the phone. It lights up with an incoming call. It's Breanna.

"Sorry, Ms. Denise, the call dropped. I'm having a problem with my connection and can barely hear you."

Yea, ok, Denise thinks.

They make arrangements for Denise to visit Breanna at noon the next day, so Denise can check out Breanna's new living arrangements which will give her enough time to write her report for next week's placement review hearing.

The thing Denise wants to do least in the world is visit Breanna, but she knows she has to, and she sincerely hopes Breanna has pulled it together for her own sake and for Tiger's. Denise starts to psyche herself up.

Denise sends an email to Rob:

"I'll be visiting with Breanna tomorrow. She might actually be doing better. Visitation with Tiger may work."

Five minutes later, Denise's computer dings. She sees a message waiting from Rob:

"Great to hear, please assess her home for cleanliness. I reviewed the file, and this was an issue at one time."

"Getting off heroin is hard," Denise says to her co-worker. "Breanna has a job, which means she has bouts of sobriety. I like that. I just hope Breanna gives me something to work with and that she really will complete rehab."

The next morning, Denise runs late to work. She kisses her daughter and watches her walk to her bus stop. Denise smiles as she hears her daughter laughing and chattering with her friends. Short for time, she takes her eighty-five-pound Golden Retriever for a walk. He doesn't seem to be pleased with his short walk, but obliges with a nice long foul smelling lump of excrement that she reaches down in the prickly, dry grass to retrieve. She ties a knot around the warm, green plastic bag. Denise hates crating him, but knows she has to because he didn't let it all out. She crates him. He whimpers and bows his head into submission as she points to the crate.

Denise's husband runs through the door saying he'd forgotten his lunch. She kisses him goodbye. "I'm two seconds behind you," she says as she shuts the door behind him.

Grabbing her car keys from the wall hook, the newspaper sitting on Denise's glass coffee table catches her eyes.

She reads the headline: "Mom of Seven Shot: Execution Style." Denise plops down in the coffee table chair and reads further. The first line reads, "Breanna McKenney, a Braxton local, was found dead last night, her arms bound behind her and a single gunshot to the back of her head."

Denise knocks a glass vase onto the floor. She tries to swallow, but the frog in her throat is just too large.

The next day, she visits Tiger at Clarissa's and gives him the news. She holds his head in her lap as he uncontrollably sobs – as he tries to figure it all out. He raises his head and then places it back down in her lap. He buries his head in her belly.

CHAPTER 21

Braxton Superior Court, Criminal Division
Thomas
August 2016

"Hung jury."

Two words Thomas never expected to hear in his criminal case.

The newest attorney in his team of lawyers, a noted expert in jury prediction, told Thomas there was an ever so slight possibility, but Thomas couldn't put faith into it.

After the first day of deliberations, three jury members wrote and signed a letter to the judge they could not, in good conscience, find Thomas guilty. The judge asked the Clerk of the Court to verify this was the case and to ask if the jurors needed any additional information. They declined and held firm in their decision.

A day later, the jury Foreman announces

the jury was unable to reach a unanimous verdict. The Jury hung. Thomas flashes to Tiger and wonders if he's okay. *Will I be able to get him back?*

After leaving court a free man, Thomas calls Dopp to see if he's heard the good news.

"Tommy Boy," Dopp answers. Thomas knows his attorney must have called him.

"What's next?" Thomas asks.

"I talked to the Bears GM, and he's thinking the Commissioner will lift your suspension based on your mistrial, July to September is long enough."

"I hear you brother, trust me, it's been a nightmare."

"How's your weight? You've been on track, right."

The corners of Thomas's mouth turn up, "Yes, man. I had nothing else to do, but be on track."

"Where ya at?" Dopp asks.

"I'm at 225 lbs, benching 350, and the last time I checked I ran a 4.5 40. I'm throwing the pigskin harder and faster."

Thomas pauses and asks, "What about that contract re-negotiation?"

"Tommy, it's not going to happen. I'm so sorry. The record may not either. That depends on the decision by the Commissioner."

"I understand," Thomas says an octave lower.

"Cheer up, Tommy boy. You're in tiptop shape, and you have time to prove yourself. Your football prowess was never ever in question, and you've got time to show all that other stuff won't distract you."

"I hear you," Thomas says

Before Thomas and Dopp hang up, Dopp asks, "How's the adoption?"

"It's not looking good," Thomas drops his head, "You know DCS removed Tiger from our home." Dopp is quiet. "We're still fighting man," Thomas says.

CHAPTER 22
Thomas and Sonya
October 2016

Thomas finds it hard to believe he's sitting on a therapist's couch in the middle of the freaken afternoon. Clean, yet worn, brown, rust and white paisley patterns cover his seat. A box emitting sounds of the ocean sits on the floor under the wooden four legged table holding two boxes of tissue. Thomas pops a mint into his mouth. Clinical accomplishments cover two of Dr. Mayfield's four walls. She comes highly recommended by the Professional Football Players Association who strongly "suggested," no demanded Thomas at least "try" therapy for the sake of contract negotiations and for the sake of restoring his brand. Funny thing is, Thomas is sort of enjoying therapy, something he, of course, would never admit out loud.

Sitting in the upright recliner to his right, Sonya interlocks her ten fingers and places them between her knees. Her hair looks more kept than it has in their past four sessions. She even has on make-up. Thomas catches himself smiling when she finds the courage to look him directly in the eyes.

Dr. Mayfield asks Thomas and Sonya to "pass the conversation stick." They'd done it before, but without success. Dr. Mayfield hands Thomas the stick and explains the rules again. "Thomas, I want you to choose a topic and make a statement about how you feel to Sonya, and then pass the stick to her," she instructs. Dr. Mayfield turns to Sonya, "Sonya, I want you to repeat back what Thomas says in your own words, and ask him if what you said was accurate, then pass him the stick," Dr. Mayfield continues. "Thomas, you then state whether what Sonya says is a precise interpretation of your thought or feeling." Thomas nods his head and takes the stick.

"Sonya when you hoed around, it made me feel devalued." Dr. Mayfield intercepts the stick exchange. "Remember our 'I' statements and think about how much more we can be heard when we alleviate statements causing defensiveness."

Thomas tries again. This time tears dart out of his eyes down to his cheeks. He tastes the salt in his mouth and the salt in his heart. Sonya begins to whimper and whimper. "Sonya, I've never been hurt as badly as I have when I found out you cheated on me." Finally, he's said it. Thomas finally said what he's wanted to say to Sonya since Greg Story showed him the photos.

Sonya grabs the stick, "I hurt you deeply when I cheated on you."

They both erupt in uncontrollable sobs.

"And my manhood, Sonya, my manhood. I've been cut to the core."

Sonya walks to the couch and wraps her arms around his neck. Thomas lets her. He cries on her shoulder. This is the first time in Thomas's life he's been able to be transparent, be vulnerable. It feels amazing.

While he is in tremendous pain, he's thankful for the cleansing the pain has begun and for the experience of new feelings.

The next week, Thomas and Sonya

return to counseling, together. Although they still live apart, they are starting to do more and more together.

"What about the adoption?" Dr. Mayfield asks.

Sonya turns to Thomas who is sitting on the couch next to her.

He grins and places his hand on top of his, "We're working on it. Our trial has been postponed until next month."

Sonya chimes in, "The juvenile court did give us visitation, and we get to see Tiger next week."

"Very good," says the counselor, "And your living situation?"

Thomas shifts in his seat, and Sonya follows.

"Thomas?" says the Dr. Mayfield.

"We're thinking about moving back in together" he says. Thomas excuses himself to go to the bathroom. He heads back a few minutes later. He opens the door. Sonya is crying.

"What'd I miss?" asks Thomas.

Looking at Sonya and softly touching her knee, the counselor tells Thomas, "Sonya and

I were just discussing the benefit of individual counseling for both you and her. There's just some things we can't uncover in couple's counseling."

Sonya chimes in, "I think it's a good idea."

"Every pain needs a voice, and that's best given individually," Dr, Mayfield asserts.

Thomas flashes to childhood pain. Sonya does too.

He agrees.

CHAPTER 23
The Adoption Decision
November 2016

The trial seems like an eternity ago. Clarissa washes her last dish and answers a call from her adoption attorney. Her favorite R&B artist softly croons from the kitchen radio and the family television loudly sounds a new reality show about adoptive families finding their biological connections. The soap suds smell like freshly squeezed lemonade.

"We did it Clarissa, you won!" announces the lawyer. "The Court refused to award the Newmans the adoption because Thomas was arrested and the stability of their marriage has come into question."

Clarissa, slightly surprised she won, drops her cell in the draining water and hope it still works as promised by all of the commercials. She quickly dries it off. "Hello, hello," Clarissa says into the phone. Her attorney continues, "The Judge sided with you. We were right, family placement is ALWAYS the best placement."

Clarissa calls Tiger into the kitchen and gives him the news. This is the last thing Tiger wants to hear. He knows she trying, but he has never felt at home with Clarissa. *Do Thomas and Sonya still love me? Will they still visit? Did they really fight for him?*

Tiger refuses to call Clarissa "Aunt" or "Mom."

Tiger can't stop the blood rushing to his head. He sees red. He needs to escape. He explodes and punches Clarissa, who's standing in front of him. He runs upstairs to his room. Before chasing after him, Clarissa calls Uncle Charlie. He tells her he's proud. Next, she calls Jeanean. "I beat the Newmans," she taunts. "You're kidding me," replies Jeanean. "You beat those rich fucks?" Clarissa hears her mother stuttering in the background, "Shee shee only won because that man went to jail." Clarissa hangs up.

She goes upstairs to see about Tiger. He's not there. The outside window is open. She waits a few minutes and then calls the police to make a report.

Two days later, there's a knock at Clarissa's door. She opens the door to find a Truant Officer on the other side. Standing on the porch beside him is Tiger with his head bowed to the ground. He lifts his head. Dried blood is caked in the left corner of his top lip.

The Officer explains that Tiger had been caught starting a fire in the neighbor's yard. He tells her about the juvenile delinquent hearing she is mandated to attend.

After the officer leaves him at the front porch, Tiger enters Clarissa's house and pushes her out of the way. Holding her now bruised arm, Clarissa swings her left fist in his direction and misses him by an inch. She tries to recall parenting techniques she's learned from her counselor over the past several months, but in that moment, nothing comes to mind.

Tiger runs upstairs.

Clarissa hears her cell ring and answers it. Denise has called to congratulate her for winning the adoption of Tiger. Denise informs her due to the finalization of her adoption, DCS has submitted a request to close Tiger's file. Clarissa wonders if Denise is familiar with truancy court, but remains silent.

Instead, she asks, "How do I undo the adoption?"

ACKNOWLEDGEMENTS

I would like to express my deepest gratitude to everyone who helped see me through this amazing book endeavor. Without your encouragement, critique and overall support, *Adopting Tiger* would not be.

In particular, I would like to thank my writing group, developmental editor Kate Stephenson, cover artist Jay Durrah, lawyer Manotti Jenkins, photographer Julie Linstruth and media consultant Scott Street Media for your substantive and technical support. I give special thanks to my family and friends for your constructive insight, in particular: Chad Johnson, Karen Henry Smith, Paeton Chavis, Gabrielle Alexander and Spencer Truesdale.

For believing in this project and for your tender heart and reviews, I give utmost appreciation to: Marc Thompson, Ebony T. Lee, Joyce Thompson-Mills, Curt Randle El, Cynthia Newman, Milt Washington, Julieanna

Huddle, Jermaine Ross, Brian Settles, Gregg Ellis, Orlena Blanchard and Andrea Moorehead.

To my husband, Troy, whose unconditional love and sacrifice has orbited me to levels unknown, I thank you!

ABOUT THE AUTHOR

Chavis Fisher has practiced law for over seventeen years and has extensive experience in domestic, foster care and step parent adoptions. She received the prestigious U.S. Congressional *Angel in Adoption* Award in 2013 for her commitment to improve the lives of children in need of permanent homes.

Chavis Fisher has worked with hundreds of foster parents, child advocates and Department of Child Services case managers, directors and attorneys throughout her legal career.

Chavis Fisher is a CASA volunteer where she advocates for abused and neglected youth and a Body Safety Advocate where she teaches elementary students physical boundaries. Chavis Fisher has worked for the Indiana University Football Program, the Indianapolis Colts and the National Football League.

In her free time, Chavis Fisher loves to read, travel and kickbox. She is most fulfilled when she is spending time with her husband.

55863684R00115

Made in the USA
San Bernardino, CA
06 November 2017